The Best Man Problem

The Best Man Problem

Mariah Ankenman

This book is a work of fiction. Names, characters, places, and incidents are the product of the author's imagination or are used fictitiously. Any resemblance to actual events, locales, or persons, living or dead, is coincidental.

Copyright © 2020 by Mariah Ankenman. All rights reserved, including the right to reproduce, distribute, or transmit in any form or by any means. For information regarding subsidiary rights, please contact the Publisher.

Entangled Publishing, LLC
10940 S Parker Rd
Suite 327
Parker, CO 80134
rights@entangledpublishing.com

Lovestruck is an imprint of Entangled Publishing, LLC.

Edited by Stacy Abrams and Judi Lauren
Cover design by Bree Archer
Cover photography by Pekic and FollowTheFlow/Getty Images

Manufactured in the United States of America

First Edition January 2020

To my very own computer geek.

Thanks for always supporting me, encouraging me, fixing the computer so I don't toss it into the wall, and making sure I have three backups at all times.

Chapter One

There are many things a woman can do the night of her best friend's wedding: A) enjoy three slices of cake because it's a celebration, B) wallow in the misery of her singledom, C) dance the night away until her new bridesmaid shoes make her feet blister, or D) hook up with an insanely hot stranger at the hotel bar.

Lilly Walsh had chosen option D.

Oh boy, did she choose D.

Okay, so she'd also picked A, because everyone knows calories don't count when it comes to wedding cake, but the other choice was the one currently freaking her out.

Last night came rushing back to her in full Technicolor. She remembered the beautiful, intimate wedding of her best friend and business partner, Pru, to the woman's lifelong friend, Finn Jamison. There had been happy tears and sad ones, mostly from the happy couple's adorable six-month-old twins, who detested their wedding attire and let everyone in the entire hotel ballroom know it.

Food had been delicious and drinks flowing. Lilly had

partaken mostly in the food because melancholy set in after one glass of champagne. As one-third owner of Mile High Happiness, Lilly was used to planning weddings and seeing others' joy, but last night had struck a deep chord. One she hadn't realized existed.

She was lonely.

After the happy couple had been sent on their way, the festivities over, the magic of the evening ended, Lilly found herself gravitating toward the hotel bar. Pathetic? Maybe, but seeing her friend exceptionally happy caused an ache inside she desperately needed to soothe. Not one for hookups; she didn't have any of those apps on her phone. She couldn't explain why she took a seat at the polished, dark wooden bar, ordered a vodka and cranberry from the bartender, and scanned the room for a friendly eye.

She'd felt like she was part of a cheesy movie cliché and nearly left, but then she spotted...*him*.

"What did the pirate say on his eightieth birthday?"

Lilly glanced up from her drink, startled to see the attractive stranger she'd locked eyes with had come over to stand beside her.

"I'm sorry, what?"

He grinned, and her heart skipped a beat. Talk about a panty-melting smile.

"What did the pirate say on his eightieth birthday?"

"Um, what?"

The stranger's smile widened as he closed one eye and swung his arm like a buccaneer. "Ayyyyy matey!"

She tilted her head in confusion.

"Get it?" the man asked. "I'm eighty. Because he's a pirate, and they say matey, which sounds like eighty, and—"

Covering her mouth, Lilly let out an unexpected laugh at the corny joke.

"Sorry." He shrugged, grin going sheepish. "I know it's a

lame joke, but you looked like you needed a little laugh." He indicated the empty chair next to her. "May I sit?"

Though he'd used the corniest pickup line she'd ever heard, Lilly had found the man funny and extremely attractive. She'd invited him to sit, where they talked until the bartender announced last call.

"Mmmmmm."

The deep rumble of the sleepy murmur vibrated along her spine, sending tingling sensations to all her good parts. Good parts the body responsible for the sound had attended to very, very thoroughly last night.

She'd done it. Prim and proper Lilly Walsh had partaken in a one-night stand.

The woman who made a list for everything from groceries to what book she was going to read next had gone off the beaten path and taken a veritable stranger to bed to have her wicked way with him.

And how ravenously wicked it had been. Perhaps it had been the anonymity or the knowledge that she would never see him again, but last night she'd let herself go in a way she never had before.

A flush heated her skin as she remembered all the ways they'd touched and tasted each other. All the inhibitions she'd left on the floor along with her midnight-blue bridesmaid dress and three-inch heels. Pride swelled in her chest at the knowledge that she'd been a veritable sex goddess, giving and receiving more pleasure than she had with any other man, ever.

Exactly half a millisecond later, her flush of pride turned into scorching embarrassment.

I slept with a stranger!

Not entirely true. She knew his name. Lincoln… something. Okay, she knew his first name. That had to count, right?

Oh dear God, I've become my mother.

Again, not entirely true. She'd only slept with Lincoln after knowing him all of two hours, not married the guy. A quick glance to the ring finger of her left hand confirmed as much. Not that she couldn't remember the evening in vivid detail.

The strong arm draped across her chest tightened as Lincoln mumbled in his sleep again. The man was a sleep talker, she'd discovered. See! She knew him…slightly.

His large palm started to drift toward her breast, caressing the sensitive skin in an unconscious manner. A yearning ache woke between her thighs, and she mentally told her lady parts to calm down. They'd gotten their fun last night. Numerous times, as she recalled.

Now a stealthy escape was in order.

Having never engaged in a hook-up-type situation before, she really didn't know the rules for this. Was she supposed to leave before he woke up? Go grab him breakfast? Wait for him to get her room service? Have another go before she hightailed it out of there?

Honestly, the last option sounded the most tempting. However, if she stayed for round two—or five, technically—she might never leave, and wouldn't that make her look pathetic and clingy? She remembered Lincoln had said something about just arriving in town to visit some friends or reconnect with friends, but whatever he'd said, it was obvious the guy wasn't local.

Not good for the long term. Long distance rarely worked.

She should leave now, before he woke up, and keep this as a nice memory she could take out on lonely nights.

Or boring nights.

Late nights.

Any and every night.

Slowly, she shifted on the bed, her body screaming in

protest as her naked flesh rubbed against the lean, hard, and equally naked body next to her.

What are you doing? You have two more condoms in your purse. Put them to good use!

She told her raging libido to stuff it and gently lifted Lincoln's arm off her chest to make her escape. He grumbled in his sleep, rolling over as she quietly slipped out of bed. Thank God he seemed to be a heavy sleeper. Now all she had to do was find her clothes, get dressed, and make a run for it.

No, that made it sound like she regretted what happened last night, and she most certainly did not. It might have been out of character for her, a bit naughty and completely off the wall, but she didn't regret it. Slight embarrassment? Sure. Regret? Not a chance.

Besides, it wasn't like anyone had to know. It could be her little secret. Her naughty little secret. A small giggle escaped her lips at that thought, and she slapped a hand over her mouth, the noise sounding incredibly loud in the silent morning air of the hotel room.

"Get the cat off the dresser. He's an orange conductor."

Wow. Heavy sleeper *and* talked nonsense in his sleep. Lincoln was just a cornucopia of interesting quirks. No. No he wasn't. He was a good time she could put in her spank bank, and that was all. Oh, crap, she had to get out of here before she did something rash like wake the man up to jump his bones again.

Glancing around, she frantically searched for her clothing. The room was slightly fuzzy due to the fact that she'd slept in her contacts. A stupid thing to do, but she'd worn them for the wedding and hadn't brought her glasses, not expecting to spend the night anywhere but at home.

Ah, there! Her dress was strewn across a chair in the corner. Hurrying over, she almost tripped on her heels at the foot of the bed. A memory of Lincoln bending her over the end of the bed, taking her from behind while she wore nothing but those shoes he erotically referred to as "Fuck Me Shoes," entered her mind. Another flush rose on her skin, but this one came with a longing. A longing she was adamant to deny if she ever wanted to get out of here. And she did. Totally. Very anxious to leave. Yup. No reason to stay.

But her gaze drifted back to the bed and the sinfully sexy man sleeping blissfully. While he lay there, without a care in the world, her mind raged with the inner battle of the century.

Stay or go?

Go. She had to go. If only because she wanted to stay so badly.

There was no future with him. He was a fling, a fun night, a walk on the wild side. Besides, the man didn't even live here. She didn't go for the long-distance thing. Lincoln was temporary, and so were they.

Hurrying over to her dress, she shoved the garment on, grateful her friend had chosen a stretchy fabric and simple cut. She didn't think she could handle a ton of buttons or zippers this morning. She grabbed her heels, opting to put them on once she left the room for stealth reasons. Now all she needed was… Crap! Where the hell were her panties?

I threw them to the wind last night. Much like my caution.

Great, deny herself a little sex and her inner voice became a raging bitch. Hadn't last night been enough? She couldn't remember the last time she'd had so many non-self-induced orgasms. Seriously, how greedy could one woman get?

She had to leave before she fell into the temptation of another round. She didn't think she could walk away from this man in the light of day.

But he's right there!

Amazing how her inner voice sounded a lot like her free-loving hippie roommate, Moira.

Giving up on the pantie search, Lilly debated writing a

note but ultimately decided against it. What the hell would she say? *Thanks for the hot night of sex*? Ew. That sounded... wrong. Last night had been much more than hot sex, anyway. She'd felt a spark, a rush of heat, an instant connection the moment she met Lincoln's pale hazel eyes across the bar. Maybe that was the reason she felt this clawing need to escape. This was supposed to be a fun one-night stand. Nothing more.

Lilly quietly grabbed her small clutch from the TV stand and slipped out the hotel room door. In less than ten minutes, a cab dropped her off at her apartment. The perks of living in the city of Denver—what had once been called the hook-up capital of Colorado—the driver didn't even glance sideways at her appearance, which she assumed screamed "walk of shame."

She walked the flight of stairs to her apartment, sliding the key in the lock and pushing the door open with a sigh of relief. Her relief, however, was short-lived as she entered the kitchen area to see her roommate sitting at the table, coffee mug in hand, sly smile on her pixie face.

"Why, Lilly Walsh," Moira Rossi said with a waggle of her pale blond eyebrows. "I do believe you were wearing that exact dress last night."

Lifting her chin, Lilly headed toward the coffee pot and the heavenly smells emanating from it. "You know it, since you were wearing the same exact dress, Mo."

"Ah, yes, but it's eight thirty in the morning, and I'm wearing my pajamas now. And slept in my own bed last night."

Of all the mornings for her night-owl friend to be awake, why did she have to choose this one?

"Could it be our dear Lilly Walsh, champion of making a man wait until date eleven, has gone and had herself a sexual liaison?"

Lilly took her time grabbing a mug and pouring a teaspoon of creamer and a dash of sugar in before filling the mug with coffee and turning to face her smug roommate. "Maybe."

"Wahoo!" Mo pumped her fists in the air. "'Walk of success'!"

Stirring the brain juice, Lilly came to sit at the table. "Don't you mean 'walk of shame'?"

"Pfft." Mo waved a hand in the air. "Hell no. A shame would be if you spent all night with Mr. Tall, Dark, and Sexy and didn't get any. I assume from your rosy complexion and satisfied glow, you got it and then some."

She had indeed. But wait. "How do you know he's tall, dark, and sexy?"

"Aha!" Mo pointed a finger. "I didn't; you just confirmed it."

Crap! Her friend was far too crafty, considering the flower-child persona she played up.

"But it doesn't matter if he was tall or short, dark or pale, muscular or had a rocking dad-bod. All that matters is he got you where you needed to go. The spark is all that matters."

She and Lincoln didn't have spark; they had burned the city down with fireworks. But even so, Lilly didn't believe in the romantic notion of soul mates the way her friends did. She, Pru, and Mo all believed everyone deserved to have their special day with the one they loved, which was why they had started Mile High Happiness, their wedding planning company. Well, that and weddings were a very lucrative business venture. The average couple spent more than twenty-eight thousand dollars on their wedding. That was a lot of money for one day, and the women tried their best to ensure all couples got the dream wedding that would kickstart their happily ever afters.

But since 40 percent of marriages ended in divorce, she

knew happily ever after wasn't for everyone. After all, her mother was currently on her fourth "soul mate."

"Lead with your heart, Lilly dear, and love will always find you."

Her mother's oft-said advice rang with the blare of a warning bell in her mind. If leading with her heart got her what her mother had—a string of bad husbands and multiple broken hearts—she'd lead with her head, thank you very much.

Love at first sight? Spark? Soul mate? These were simply words people invented to excuse their rash decision to jump into huge, life-altering changes too soon. She'd seen it before. A couple so enamored with each other they couldn't see the problems ahead for the stars in their eyes. Mark her words, those who rushed in would rush right back out when they discovered that spark didn't last.

You had to have substance, compatibility. You couldn't just see someone and know. Love didn't work that way.

"Are you seeing him again?"

Only in her dreams.

"I highly doubt it. He's from out of town."

Mo gasped, placing a hand to her heart. "Your first one-night stand. Oh, my precious Lil. I'm so proud of you. Look at you stretching your sexual wings."

That didn't even make sense.

"I can't wait to tell Pru when she gets back from her honeymoon."

"Don't you dare!" She might have enjoyed last night, but she didn't want to go broadcasting it to the world. *Attention, all! Lilly Walsh slept with a man whose last name she doesn't even know.* Might as well start wearing clothes fifteen years too young for her and becoming her mother now. "This was an impulsive, one-time thing induced by an overwhelming mix of emotions at seeing my best friend get married to the man she loves."

"Hey!" Mo stuck her bottom lip out. "I thought I was your best friend."

"What, are we in grade school? A person can have more than one best friend, Moira."

"Then say it."

She sighed, knowing the tiny woman wasn't going to give up until she did as commanded. "You are also my best friend."

A huge smile crossed the woman's face, blond curls—streaked with blue in homage to the wedding colors—bouncing as she rose from her seat to cross to Lilly and envelop her in an exuberant hug. Lilly patted her back, always unsure how to respond to her friend's overt displays of affection.

"I know. I just like hearing you say it."

"Yeah, yeah." She stood, extricating herself from the emotional display. "I'm going to take a shower and change into something more comfortable."

"Ooooh, is that what you said to Mr. Sexy last night?"

Her face flamed. "Mo!"

"Oh, calm down. I promise your walk on the wild side is safe with me. No one but me and your showerhead will ever know."

"Why do I live with you again?"

"Because you love me and I let you take the last of the coffee," Mo said as she finished pouring the pot into Lilly's mug. "Now go take that shower. Remember, we share it, so maybe try not pleasuring yourself to the memories of last night's sexcapades."

She was going to need a second job, since her rent would increase soon, due to the fact that she was going to kill her roommate.

"Oh, stop staring daggers at me and go." Mo blew her a kiss. "Have fun! I'll just scrub the shower down later."

Shaking her head, she moved down the hall without argument, but only because a nice, steamy shower sounded like heaven right about now. She would most certainly not be thinking about Lincoln and his amazing hands, tongue, and—dammit! No. She had her fun, and now it was over. Time to get back on track.

No pining over a hot one-night stand that could never go anywhere. She had a business to run, friends she loved, and maybe, if there were time, she would search out a suitable man who fit into her life. A compatible one. Someone she could depend on.

That was key. Not sparks. After all, sparks started fires, and fires could destroy your entire world.

Chapter Two

"Hey, Lil." Moira rose from her small desk in the corner of their office. "I'm going to head out to grab some lunch. You wanna come?"

Lilly glanced up from the yellow folder she had open on her desk. "Can't. Kenneth and Marie will be here in ten minutes."

"Oh right, the Buller-Lin wedding." Mo's nose wrinkled. "Did we have a meeting with them scheduled for today?"

"No. Marie texted me this morning asking if they could come in for a quick minute."

The woman had sounded a bit harried but not as frantic as some brides tended to be. Lilly liked Marie and Kenneth. So much so that after the sweet couple insisted on her calling them by their first names at their initial meeting seven months ago, she'd complied. Normally she preferred to keep a strictly professional relationship. Especially after "the incident." But the charming couple who owned and ran a small coffee shop in the Santa Fe arts district were so genuinely kind, she hadn't been able to deny their request.

"I hope nothing is wrong."

She did, too, but even if something terrible had occurred to derail their dream wedding, Mile High Happiness could handle it. Lilly wasn't worried. In fact, she thrived on solving problems. Wedding-related problems. For other people.

Her own problems? That was another story entirely.

"I'm sure everything is fine. Marie didn't sound too stressed."

"Good." Mo stood, grabbing her patchwork tote and slipping it over her shoulder. "That poor woman deserves every bit of happiness life can throw her way."

When people came to them, in love, giddy about joining their life to their soul mate's, they tended to share their life stories. Sometimes the job felt like being a part-time therapist. Lilly had heard hundreds of proposal stories over the years—it was the first question they generally asked a prospective couple. Some made her laugh, some made her smile, a few made her cringe, and almost all of them made her shed a happy tear or two. But Marie and Kenneth had been put through the ringer—involving Marie's battle with a vicious cancer that almost took her from this world—and come out more in love than ever.

They were a true love story and a joy to be around.

"Do you need me to stay for the meeting?"

She waved a hand, pushing her glasses up as they slipped down the bridge of her nose. "No, but bring me back a sub, will you?"

"Ham and cheese, double the cheese?"

"You know me so well."

Mo winked, blowing her a kiss as she left their office. Lilly turned back to the folder that contained all the details for Kenneth and Marie's upcoming nuptials. They were down to the wire. A month away. The only items left were a few fittings, dance rehearsals, and the pre-wedding parties. Not much could go wrong now.

Way to jinx yourself, Lilly.

She took a settling breath, knowing she would do whatever she could to help her clients, as the door swung open again and Marie's smiling face popped in.

"Hey, Lilly."

"Marie." Returning the infectious smile, she stood, motioning for the woman to enter. "Come on in. Where's Kenneth?"

Oh God, please don't let this sweet, wonderful woman say they'd called it off. She swore if that man had done anything to hurt Marie, Lilly would use her prized Kate Spade heels to create some very painful new orifices in his body.

"He's parking the car with our best man. He didn't want me slipping on the ice in the parking lot, so he let me out at the front door."

Of course Kenneth would look out for her. How could Lilly think differently? The man clearly cherished the ground Marie walked on. You could see it in the way he stared at the woman he loved. With pure, unfiltered adoration. Sometimes it hurt to see, because a small, ugly, jealous part of Lilly ached to have a man glance at her with even an ounce of the love Kenneth showed Marie. He would never put her in danger, not even inadvertently, by letting her take a risky walk on the ice. January in Colorado meant cold temperatures and wet snow, the perfect storm for black ice. Lilly had already almost eaten it three times this week on the slippery sidewalks of the city.

"Can I get you some coffee or tea while we wait for them?"

"No thanks." The small woman with the closely cropped jet-black hair took a seat in one of the plush chairs facing Lilly's desk. "Thank you for seeing us today on such short notice. We won't keep you long, I promise. We just wanted to stop by and introduce you to our best man."

"Oh?" Lilly retook her seat as well.

"Yeah, with the shop being so busy right now and us planning on taking a week off for our honeymoon, we're trying like mad to train our weekend manager, Max, to handle any emergency that might arise during our absence, so our friend agreed to come out a month early and pitch in with any wedding stuff we needed in case we can't make a meeting or something."

"Not a problem. We often deal with various members of the wedding party. If he has your approval, then Mile High Happiness is happy to work with him."

Better a best man than a momzilla. People often thought brides were the worst, but after eight years in the business, Lilly knew the real PITAs were the mothers.

"Oh good, because he has carte blanche as far as we're concerned. We've all been friends for years. He was my lab partner in college. In fact, that's how Kenneth and I met. They were roommates, and one night we were studying in the dorm. Kenneth came in with pizza, and boom!"

Lilly felt her lips curl up in a smile. "Love at first sight?"

"Duh. The guy had pizza!" Marie laughed.

Lilly joined in with a chuckle of her own. "Yes, I say any man who brings you food is one worth keeping." Especially if that food came in a cheese variety.

"Anyway, we were the three musketeers after that. Been best friends ever since." A blush rose on the pale woman's cheeks. "Well, more than friends for Kenneth and me, obviously."

Warmth filled Lilly's chest. Yet another reason to love this couple. Marie's story of college friendship lasting the years reminded her of her own college roommates, who were also her business partners. She, Mo, and Pru had all met freshman year, and though the three women were very different, they formed a bond nothing could break. They were more than friends. They were sisters—sisters of the heart.

"Well then, I cannot wait to meet him."

"They should be..." Marie turned in her seat to face the door. "Oh, here come Kenneth and Lincoln now."

Lincoln? A small sense of trepidation filled her belly, but she shrugged it off. No. It couldn't be. Lincoln was a pretty common name, wasn't it? She was simply projecting because last weekend had been so amazing.

Lilly glanced up, the smile on her face faltering, the warmth in her chest freezing into an icy cold block of panic, because as Kenneth walked through the door, heading straight for his fiancée, the man behind him came into startling, horrifying focus.

Dark brown hair, pale hazel eyes, more than a hint of dark scruff along his sharp jaw, and sinfully full lips. Lips she vividly remembered caressing every inch of her body just last weekend...

Oh shit!

Lincoln No-last-name. Her one and only one-night stand.

Why couldn't it have been a momzilla?

· · ·

Lincoln Reid stopped short two feet into the office of his best friends' wedding planner. *Well I'll be damned.* If it wasn't the woman who'd blown his mind—along with other parts of his anatomy—and then blown out of his life before he could grab her number. Lilly No-last-name. What were the odds? He had a math minor; he should know. Whatever the odds were, he didn't care. He was just happy to see her again. When he'd woken up satisfied but alone in his hotel room a week ago, a keen sense of loss had poured through him.

Sure, they hadn't made any promises or even exchanged

personal details, but he'd been hoping Lilly would want to repeat their amazing night together. He knew he sure did.

"Lilly Walsh, this is our friend and best man, Lincoln Reid." Marie stood, cuddling up to Kenneth's side as she made the introduction.

Lincoln opened his mouth to inform his friends he was already acquainted with their wedding planner—intimately, but they didn't need to know that much—when he noticed the infinitesimal shake of Lilly's head and the pure panic in her bright green eyes. So she recognized him as well but didn't want Marie or Kenneth to know.

Ouch.

Couldn't say that didn't sting, but he wasn't the type to ignore a lady's wishes. Even if they weren't spoken—more like screamed at him with her eyes.

He quickly changed course, smiling as if he'd never met the woman before in his life. Hadn't seen every beautiful, perfect inch of her naked body. Didn't know the sweet moans she made when reaching completion.

"Hi, Lilly. Nice to meet you."

"Lovely to meet you too, Mr. Reid."

Ooooh, *Mr. Reid*. He liked the sound of that. Maybe he could convince her to say it again when they were naked and— Whoa! He needed to put thoughts like that on the back burner or he was going to test the strength of the zipper on these jeans. Besides, it seemed Ms. Walsh didn't want anyone to know of their liaison. Why would he assume she'd be open to another round?

"We just wanted you two to meet in case—" Marie was interrupted by the loud peal of "Cake by the Ocean." His friend sighed, pulling her phone from her purse and grimacing at Kenneth. "It's Max. Sorry," she addressed Lilly. "We have to take this, but it won't be more than a few minutes."

His friends hurried out of the office, leaving him and

Lilly alone.

Perfect.

He smiled at the woman who had taken her seat and was suddenly extremely absorbed in whatever paperwork was contained in the file on her desk. He took a seat in the plush high-back chair in front of her.

"So, Lilly," he began, not deterred in the slightest when she refused to look up. "Was I that bad?"

Now she glanced up, a confused expression filling her green eyes. "Huh?"

He shrugged. "I must have been a pretty shitty lover for you to run out on me before the sun rose, no goodbye kiss, no note, not even a complimentary coffee."

Her eyes narrowed behind black, thick-rimmed cat-eye glasses. She hadn't been wearing glasses the night they met. Though she had been wearing a fancy dress, the kind one might wear for a wedding. Perhaps she'd worn contacts for the festive occasion. She looked great either way, but he liked the glasses. It brought attention to her amazing gem-like eyes. And paired with the bright white button-up blouse and dark pencil skirt she wore, it gave her the look of a woman in power. A sexy woman in power.

He always did enjoy strong women.

"The sun was up when I left, I assure you. I can't help it if you laze about all day. And the hotel gives every guest complimentary coffee."

"What about the note?"

Some of her pique dissipated, pearly white teeth biting down on her plump, siren-red bottom lip in a seriously sexy move he knew was in no way intended to be one. A small amount of guilt filled her gaze.

"I am sorry for not saying goodbye, but honestly"—she took a deep breath, letting it out before continuing—"that was my first one-night stand, and I wasn't sure of the rules."

He leaned forward, placing an arm on her desk. "Can I confess a secret? It was mine, too."

She raised one dark brow as if she didn't believe him. Let her think what she wanted. He hadn't had sex with a woman in over two years before Lilly. Probably one of the reasons why her disappearing act hit him so hard that morning.

"Hmm, well, I am sorry if I hurt your feelings in any way."

Hurt his feelings was a bit much. Wounded his pride? Sure, but she couldn't hurt his feelings. No woman could do that anymore. Lincoln had made sure of it.

"You're forgiven." He leaned back in the chair again. "How about you make it up to me by letting me take you out to dinner tomorrow night?"

Her face got that panicked look again. Damn, he did not like seeing it there.

"Oh, no, I can't... I, um, I don't engage in relationships with clients."

Solid rule, considering her clients were couples about to plunge into wedded bliss, but...

"I never said anything about a relationship." He'd been there, done that, got the broken heart and divorce papers to prove it. Not doing that shit again. "It's just dinner. And I'm not your client." Marie and Kenneth were.

"Yes, but you're a part of the wedding party, and we have a strict rule at Mile High Happiness not to fraternize with any member of an active wedding party."

Did that mean they could *fraternize* all they wanted once Marie and Kenneth said "I Do"?

He chose to save that question for later because he figured he knew the answer she would give right now, and it wasn't the one he wanted to hear. He was saved from asking anything further when the office door swung open to reveal his friends.

"Sorry about that." Marie laughed, holding up her phone.

"Max is a great manager, but I think he's stressing out about us being gone for a week. He's on a trial run by himself this morning and freaking at every little thing that goes wrong."

"I understand." Lilly smiled at his friends.

"Did you guys get to know each other?"

Lincoln barked out a laugh, quickly morphing the sound into a cough at the death glare from Lilly. "Um, yeah. Little bit."

"Great!"

"We should really be getting back to the shop, sweetheart." Kenneth wrapped an arm around Marie's waist, nuzzling her ear with his lips.

He loved his friends, but sometimes their happiness felt like a dagger being plunged straight into his heart. What happened with him and Jessa wasn't their fault. But he'd learned his lesson. Falling in love and giving someone that kind of power wasn't something he wanted.

His gaze traveled back to the woman sitting across from him, his mind conjuring up memories of her smooth skin, flush and glistening with sweat as she rode him hard, dark hair loose and flying down her back like a shadowy waterfall.

Lust. Now that was something he trusted. And Lilly might be able to deny a lot of things about them, but he'd bet every penny he had that, before this wedding was over, the sensual woman wouldn't be able to deny that together, they were explosive.

Chapter Three

Somehow, Lilly managed to last another ten minutes in Lincoln, Marie, and Kenneth's presence until the trio said their goodbyes, mentioning something about seeing her at the final tux fitting in a few days. Honestly, she could barely hear past the booming voice in her head.

You slept with the best man!
Again!

How stupid could one woman be?

That wasn't entirely fair. Technically she hadn't known Lincoln was the best man for Marie and Kenneth's wedding. How could she have known he'd be acquainted with her current wedding clients? It's not like she walked around with a questionnaire for prospective one-night stands. She never had one-night stands in the first place.

She'd never been so glad for a slow season. Since it was January, they were done with all the holiday-themed weddings, and things wouldn't really pick back up until spring, so the only wedding she had to focus on at the moment was this one. No way could she handle another. Not when she *slept with the best man...again.*

The line kept repeating in her head, an annoying earworm she couldn't shake. The polite smile seemed frozen to her face, hurting her cheeks with the forced, contented expression she couldn't for the life of her drop. They were gone now. She could unclench, relax, even freak out if she wanted to. Then why was she still standing behind her desk, placid grin stretching her lips, internal screaming going full blast?

"Hey." Mo pushed her way through the office door, glancing into the plastic bag in her hands. "They didn't have any salt and vinegar chips left, so I got you BBQ. I hope that's—"

"Lincoln was here!" Okay then, apparently all it took to bring her out of her funk into full flip-out mode was her best friend giving a non-threatening colloquial greeting.

Mo stopped short, long bohemian skirt swishing back and forth with the abruptness of her motion. Her head tilted up, blond and blue curls bouncing off her shoulders with the movement. Two pale eyebrows rose as light, honey-colored eyes widened.

"Okay...who's Lincoln?"

"My one-night stand!" Was she shouting? She felt like she was shouting. Why couldn't she stop shouting?

Mo placed the hand not holding the food to her heart. "Aww, he found you. That's either super romantic or supremely creepy." Her best friend took a moment to think it over. "I'm going to vote for romantic."

Of course she would. Because Mo thought everything in life was sunshine and rainbows. Even villains had a heart of gold if you dug deep enough, and everyone had a soul mate they eventually found and lived happily ever after with, according to Moira Rossi. Her childlike optimism was sweet but could be slightly frustrating at times. Times like this, when the situation was neither romantic nor creepy but simply one on the precipice of utter ruin.

"It's fate." Her friend and business partner hurried forward, setting the bag of food on Lilly's desk, a wide grin dominating her small, round face. "He's your one. Your soul mate."

Nonsense. Lilly didn't believe in soul mates. Good matches, sure. Partners in life, absolutely, but something as silly as fated loves? No. Lasting love was built on respect and common ground. Not fairy tales.

"No, Moira, he's not my soul mate, and he didn't come looking for me. He's Marie and Kenneth's best man."

"Huh, small world."

When the short woman said nothing more, Lilly lifted her hands to emphasize her point.

"Their best man. As in a member of the wedding party."

"I know what a best man is, Lil," she said, pulling out a bag of sour cream and onion chips and opening them.

How could she casually eat chips at a time like this? When the figurative sky could come crashing down on their heads at any moment? Again!

"And I slept with him."

Mo stared at her, crunching the chip she'd just placed in her mouth before sliding her hand in the bag and pulling out another, offering it to Lilly.

"Chip?"

"How can you eat at a time like this?"

Mo glanced at the clock on the wall. "You mean lunchtime?"

That's it. She really *was* going to kill her roommate. She'd have to take up ride-share driving or work nights at a bar making enough tips to cover the entire rent, because Mo was being intentionally obtuse about this very real, very serious situation. The woman drove her mad sometimes. If she didn't love her so much—

"Did he forget your name or act like he didn't remember you?"

"No."

She shifted on her feet. Quite the opposite, in fact. The moment they locked eyes, Lilly saw the surprise and happiness light up those green-and-golden-hazel depths. She'd been the one to quash any and all admittance of former acquaintance. Lincoln had acquiesced to her silent plea, but the happy spark in his eyes dimmed the moment she pretended not to know him.

And now she felt guilty. Perfect.

"Was his wife or girlfriend with him?"

She shook her head. "He said he was single when I met him at the bar."

But she'd been lied to before by a man. A best man.

"Oh, sweetie." Mo, the amazing friend she was, picked up on Lilly's thoughts and rushed around the desk to her side. "What happened before wasn't your fault."

"I had a relationship with a married man." The words fell out of her on a shamed whisper. She feared that if she spoke them loud enough, the whole world would hear and judge her for her foolish mistake. "And almost ruined our business."

"No, you dated a lying slimeball who told you he was single and whose slimeball family took his side when he claimed you seduced him because all they could see was a charming prince when we all know him for the toad he really was."

None of that changed the fact that he had been married. Which made Lilly the other woman, the homewrecker, the tart. She'd been sick for months over what she'd inadvertently done. The damage it caused, not only to her business and a poor woman's marriage but also to her heart. Trust wasn't something Lilly gave easily, now even doubly so.

"I have a…difficult time letting go of mistakes. I admit that."

"Really." Mo raised a single eyebrow, a sardonic smile tilting her lips. "I wonder why that is."

Though the women had only met in college, she, Mo, and Pru had shared everything about their childhoods over many late-night study sessions and mountains of cheesecake. Her friends knew Lilly grew up watching her mother move from one bad mistake to another. Always flitting from man to man in hopes that this one would be the real deal. But they never were. And eventually her mother would dump the guy's ass or be left heartbroken—and occasionally broke, the few times a con man had grifted them.

"Look." Mo tilted her head. "All I'm saying is, if you like this guy, if you had a connection that might turn into something more, why not go for it?"

Because last time she "went for it," she made a huge judgment error, and they got sued and almost lost everything. Lincoln was supposed to be a one-time thing. One wild night she could look back on in her old age and say to herself, *See, Lilly, you stepped out of the box a time or two. You were adventurous and passionate once.* She could be that woman; she simply chose not to because she knew what passion did.

It died.

A horrible, ugly death that usually resulted in screaming, crying, divorce, being packed up to move to yet another crappy apartment, and starting at a new school in the middle of the year again.

"He's a client, Mo. He's off-limits."

"He's a friend of the client."

Lilly ignored Mo, reaching across the desk for her sandwich. She wasn't particularly hungry—not with her stomach still flip-flopping like a fish out of water—but she needed something besides her starry-eyed, sentimental roommate to focus on.

"And isn't off-limits code for forbidden fruit?"

"It's forbidden for a reason, Mo."

"Yeah, because it's hot."

Taking her seat, she glanced up. "How can fruit be hot?"

Mo let out a long-suffering sigh, the kind Lilly usually made when regarding the other woman. She had to say: it did not feel good to be on the receiving end.

"We're not talking about fruit, and you know it, Lilly Walsh." Mo leaned back against the desk. "So, tell me. Is Lincoln hot?"

"Hot" would be an understatement for the pure magnetic power of that man.

"We have work to do, Moira."

"Ha! He *is* hot. Smoking hot, I bet."

And then some. Taking her silence as confirmation, Mo grabbed her own sandwich out of the plastic bag and headed to her small desk at the far end of the office. Lilly scarfed down her ham and cheese in less than ten minutes. She tended to stress eat, which was why she also finished off her entire bag of chips and four squares of chocolate from her emergency stash hidden in the bottom drawer of her desk.

Damn Lincoln and his stupid, sexy face. Everything had been fine an hour ago, when all she had of him were fond memories and a tiny bit of regretful longing. Now she had to deal with keeping their liaison a secret lest it upset her clients and find some way to tell her stupid, horny body to calm down. Because whenever the man got within two feet of her, all her good parts screamed out for a second time.

Nope. Not happening.

Thankfully, Mo let the subject drop. For now. Lilly would put money on her nosy roomie asking about Lincoln before the week was through. But for now, they finished the workday in relative peace.

After they shared dinner in their apartment just one floor above their office—best commute in the city—Mo went to her weekly pub quiz at City Tavern, and Lilly spent the night bingeing her favorite cooking show, in which the contestants tried to recreate top-chef desserts and failed—hard. It always put her in a good mood, because the host was hilarious and Lilly baked about as well as the poor people on the show.

Lucky for her and her habit of stress eating, her business gave her access to all the best bakeries in Denver. Mile High Happiness was always receiving sample cakes and desserts from local bakeries that wanted to get in the wedding business. If a business owner dropped off a red velvet cake, chocolate-dipped strawberries, and berry whipped parfaits, she had to sample the goods. It was her job. She couldn't very well recommend a bakery to a client if she didn't fully support their products.

That was just bad business.

Ten o'clock rolled around. Did it make her old if she went to bed now? Used to be, the evening wouldn't even get started until ten thirty. But for a woman soon to celebrate the one-year anniversary of her twenty-ninth birthday, staying up until two in the morning held little appeal anymore. Let Mo the night owl do that. Lilly preferred her beauty sleep.

After stuffing the last of the fluffy and heavenly sweet red velvet cake in her mouth, Lilly placed her dirty plate and empty glass of milk in the dishwasher and headed to her room to get ready for bed. But even her calming nightly routine of a soothing facemask, fifteen minutes of meditation, and her ultra-cozy fleece jammies couldn't settle her whirling brain. With no TV as a distraction, the stupid thing kept circling back to today and Lincoln.

How the hell was she going to get through the next month until Marie and Kenneth's wedding if she had to be around her far-too-tempting one-night stand? Maybe she'd get lucky and wouldn't have to see much of him. After all, there were only a few more meetings and things she had to work on with the couple. Perhaps Lincoln wouldn't be at every one. And the ones he did attend, she simply had to remain professional. She could do that.

Is it professional to want to strip him and eat wedding cake off his naked body?

Crap!

She was in so much trouble. There had to be something she could do to squash this ridiculous attraction she felt for the man. But what? Tossing and turning in her bed, she knew sleep would elude her until she came up with a solution. She threw back her fluffy Sherpa blanket and she sat up in bed, reaching for the notebook and pen on her nightstand. Since solutions to problems often hit her in the middle of the night, she kept the pair by her bedside at all times. Saved her ass more than once.

"Okay," she spoke out loud in the silent room. "Let's make a list."

A siren sounded outside her window, but, having lived in the city for most of her life, she'd learned to block the noise out as she wrote. She made two columns, one with her name and one with Lincoln's. Under her name she filled out her likes, dislikes, goals in life, dreams for the future. Under Lincoln's name...huh. Honestly, beyond his name and friendship with Marie and Kenneth, she didn't know much about the man.

"Likes?" She knew he liked it when she took charge in the bedroom and he groaned in pleasure when she— Whoa. Back that train of thought up right now. She was trying to dissuade herself from any further sexy-time thoughts of the man, not prime herself for another night of naughty dreams starring Lincoln Reid.

She could do this. There had to be something. Racking her brain, she remembered one small detail Marie had said.

The woman had mentioned Lincoln coming out to help, and she had met the man at a hotel. From that information, she could infer he didn't live in Denver or anywhere within close driving distance.

"Ha!"

Something—not a lot, but big enough to put a halt to any thoughts of continuing a relationship with him. Lilly wanted a partner in life, someone to come home to every night. Couldn't do that with a man who lived...wherever he lived.

"Long distance," she wrote under Lincoln's name. She glanced at the paper. Her column filled all the way down the page, and his had only one thing written. "One fact, but an important fact."

"I never said anything about a relationship. It's just dinner."

Lincoln's earlier words rang in her memory. The man clearly had an issue with commitment. The way he'd grimaced just saying the word "relationship"...he had to be a short-term-type guy.

Strike two!

Lilly may not believe in true love, but she did believe in lasting, committed partnerships. Contrary to what Lincoln might think of her from their one night together, she was not a one-and-done-type woman. Opposite relationship goals was going on the list.

There. They didn't match on paper, so he couldn't be a good match for her. Satisfied with her logic, she placed the notebook and pen back on the bedside table and slipped under the covers again. Frantic brain sated, she slipped into a peaceful slumber. And if she had naughty dreams about Lincoln, that was fine, because dreams were not reality. And in real life, Lincoln Reid was all wrong for her.

Chapter Four

"Dude." Kenneth shot Lincoln a skeptical glance as he readjusted the moving box in his arms. "This is the fourth box labeled *computer parts*. Are you building Skynet or something?"

Lincoln hefted his own box, also labeled *computer parts*—dammit—and pushed past his friend. "That doesn't even make sense. Skynet is a self-aware worldwide neural network. I'd need more than a few boxes of hard drives and RAM."

"You are such a nerd."

"Whatever, hipster."

Kenneth glanced quickly over his shoulder as the two men carefully maneuvered their hauls down the stairs. "Just because I own a coffee shop doesn't make me a hipster."

"*Dude.*" Lincoln shook his head. "You own a coffee shop that only uses fair-trade beans, you only sell organic pastries, you play the banjo, and you have a unicycle."

"The unicycle is an heirloom from my grandfather. I can't actually ride the thing. And banjos are awesome."

He chuckled at his friend's indignation. "Still a hipster."

"Hey, Marie!" Kenneth called out as the men entered the basement apartment. "Can we call the landlord and take back our recommendation of Lincoln?"

"Boys, stop fighting or I'm not making my famous margaritas tonight," Marie answered from the depths of the apartment.

"We're sorry," they answered in unison.

Giving his best friend shit was a luxury he hadn't had in years, since Kenneth and Marie moved from Nebraska to Colorado, but he wasn't willing to risk missing out on Marie's delicious—and potent—margaritas. Her promise to make them weekly was half the reason he decided to move out here. Okay, not really, but it had been a plus.

The forces of sheer luck and utter frustration had combined to push Lincoln to make the move. His job had been going nowhere, and Nebraska held nothing but bad memories. As a software engineer, he could pretty much find work anywhere, but Silicon Valley and San Francisco—where the mega-high-paying work was—were too expensive, even for his skill set. Over the past decade, Denver had become the new hot spot for up-and-coming tech companies, so when an opportunity in the Mile High City presented itself, he'd jumped on it. Lucky for him, his best buds knew of a place to rent that wouldn't blow his budget—Denver might not be the City by the Bay, but rent was still pricey, as he'd come to find out—and it happened to be close to his friends.

Very close.

"How thick is this ceiling?" Lincoln placed his box on the floor, eyeing his friend. "And please tell me your bedroom isn't right above mine."

Kenneth and Marie lived in a charming two-bedroom Craftsman-style bungalow right by Wash Park. The basement of the house was a one bedroom complete with tiny kitchen and three-quarter bath. Perfect for a lone person. That lone person being him. The previous tenant was supposed to move out last week, but due to a delay of paperwork on his new place, he had to stay a few days. Lincoln, being the laid-back guy he was, decided to crash in a hotel while the sweet older gentleman settled his affairs. His friends had offered to let him stay with them in the interim, but one night in college still haunted his dreams.

In his defense, there hadn't been a sock or tie or anything on the door—hell, it hadn't even been locked. How was he supposed to know if he went into *his* room that his eyes would be subjected to sights he could never unsee? Namely the naked, bronzed, hairy ass of his best friend. Thank God Marie had been obscured by Kenneth and the sorry excuse for sheets they'd tried to cover themselves with. He didn't know if he could have ever looked her in the eye again if he'd accidently seen her naked. As it was, he still had to wash the image of Kenneth's butt out with a good strong drink every now and then.

After that night, they instilled a strict policy. No nookie without warning the roommate. And he never intended to have that problem again. No roommates? No accidental ass viewings.

Besides, if he hadn't chosen to stay in a hotel, he never would have met Lilly.

Not true, dumbass. You met her yesterday.

Yeah, and she wanted to pretend they didn't know each other. Ouch.

"Mr. Stottlemire never complained about any noises." Kenneth shrugged.

Marie came into the room from the small bathroom. "Mr. Stottlemire was fifty percent deaf in both ears. He wore hearing aids that didn't work and loved us because we always brought him leftover apple turnovers from the shop. He wouldn't have complained even if we had stomped around like a herd of elephants."

Lincoln didn't care about loud feet. His friends could tap dance for all he cared. As long as they kept other *activities* from drifting down to his poor ears.

"Lincoln, I unpacked your toiletries and set them all up for you."

"Babe." Kenneth wrapped an arm around his fiancée. "You weren't supposed to unpack anything."

"You guys won't let me carry any boxes. How else was I supposed to help?"

He smiled. "Thanks, Marie, but you don't need to help at all. You were the one who convinced the landlord he should rent to me when there were five other people putting in offers on this place. You did enough. You're awesome."

She raised one dark eyebrow. They all knew why Kenneth was so insistent his fiancée didn't do any heavy lifting. Though she'd been in remission for a year, the cancer that almost took Marie's life had scared them all and taken strength she was still trying to regain.

"I know I'm awesome. I've been saying it for years."

He laughed along with her and Kenneth. The cancer might have taken her strength, health, and nearly her life, but damn if it hadn't been able to take away her spunk. He'd never gotten a better call in his life than the day Marie and Kenneth rang to inform him she'd gotten the all clear from the doc. He'd been elated for her—and Kenneth. The guy had been a massive wreck from the moment she'd been diagnosed. But those two stuck together through thick and thin. They'd already seen sickness; now he hoped their marriage would be filled with a lifetime of happiness and health.

Someone's should be.

He shook off the morose thought. He was here for Marie and Kenneth and new beginnings. Not to wallow in the crap show that had been *his* love life. It had been two years since Jessa left. Time to move the fuck on. That's why he was here. New state, new life.

"Was that the last of the boxes?"

He nodded at her question.

"When are they picking the pod up?"

"I'll call the company tonight. They should be grabbing it before morning. Is it okay in the driveway for that long?"

Kenneth shrugged. "It's fine. Street sweeping day isn't until Tuesday. The cars will be okay parked on the street another night."

Great. He was here. All moved in—mostly. He still had a lot of unpacking to do, but this was it. He had a new job starting in a few weeks, a place to live right under his best friends, and a woman who was fascinating to figure out. *Lilly Walsh*. Just thinking her name made his heart beat faster. She might want to pretend they never met, but he'd seen the racing of her pulse, heard the uptake of her breath. She remembered every detail of their night together.

Fondly, he could only hope.

It was the best damn night he'd had in a long time.

"I believe the proper payment for helping a friend move in is pizza and beer." He dug his phone out of his pocket. "Should I order in, or do we go out?"

"Let's order in." Marie snuggled into Kenneth's arms. "There's a great local place on Broadway that delivers."

"They deliver beer, too?"

"Sadly, no, but I think…" She turned her head to look up at Kenneth. "Babe, do you still have that new lager we got from Renegade?"

One thing Lincoln had learned in his short time in the city: small craft breweries were a dime a dozen. Denver was a hops lover's paradise.

"Yeah, I think so. You two order the pizza. I'll go check."

Kenneth kissed his fiancée on the cheek and headed up the stairs, calling over his shoulder, "No pineapple!"

"Got it. Extra pineapple." Lincoln laughed as his friend flipped him off behind his back, disappearing out the door. "The man has terrible taste in pizza, Marie. I can't understand why you're marrying him."

She nudged him with her shoulder. "Not everyone appreciates the finer delicacies in life, like pineapple pizza, but I can forgive him and his uncultured palate because he's got a huge—"

"Ahhh! Stop right there before I have to wash my ears out with acid."

"Heart, pervert. I was going to say heart."

Sure she was. Marie might look all sweet and delicate, but the woman had the sense of humor of a twelve-year-old boy.

"Uh-huh."

"Oh, shut up and give me your phone. I'll download the pizza place app for you."

He handed over his phone, contemplating how to word what he wanted to ask her as she downloaded the pizza app.

"Lilly seems nice. I mean, I've never met a wedding planner before, but she was friendly."

Marie didn't look up from what she was doing, but a smile tilted her lips. "She is. She came highly recommended by a regular customer who worked with her for her wedding. All the women of Mile High Happiness are great."

"It's more than just Lilly?" He should have guessed. Running a business was hard, as his friends always liked to say—doing it alone would be almost impossible.

"Yeah, she runs it with her two best friends, Moira and Prudence. Mo is a hoot, and Pru has the most adorable little twins. She had them in the office one day, and I got to hold them."

He smiled at the joy in his friend's voice. "Sounds like you know the women well."

She handed his phone back, pizza app downloaded and opened. "We've bonded over a coffee here and there. I've spent the most time with Lilly, though; she's the one who handles all the client requests, she says."

He stared at the menu, glancing through the pizza selection. "Makes sense. She's a very take-charge kind of person."

"Huh?"

At Marie's mutter of confusion, he realized his mistake. "I mean, she seems that way. From what I saw meeting her the other day."

"Hmm, and what *did* you see?"

He kept his eyes firmly on his phone. Had to concentrate on his order. Pizza selection was a very serious business. "What? Oh, nothing much. I just met her."

Not true, but if Lilly wanted to keep their previous meeting a secret, he would respect that. Didn't mean he wouldn't remember it, dream of it, and fantasize about it happening again. But he wasn't some kind of asshole who shared intimate stories of his sexual exploits.

"Really?"

Crap. He'd forgotten Marie had a bullshit meter a mile wide. The woman could always tell when someone was lying. Too damn bad. He wasn't spilling anything. He glanced up from his phone to stare his friend directly in her dark, knowing eyes.

"Veggie lover's okay? You're still not eating meat, right?"

She crossed her arms over her chest. "Yes and yes."

They stared at each other in silence. Ha! That trick might work on her loving fiancé, but not on him. Lincoln's cousin, Aimee, used to pull the silent treatment on him all the time. Immune.

"I got beer!"

Hallelujah! Saved by the beer.

He pressed the order button on his phone, grinning at Marie. "Pizza's ordered."

She cocked her head to indicate this conversation wasn't over but dropped it for the moment in favor of accepting a beer and kiss from her future husband.

"You guys wanna play some Smash Up while we wait for the pizza?" Kenneth held the tabletop game he'd brought down with the drinks.

Lincoln took a beer and headed with his friends to his small kitchen table that would probably also be his desk until he bought a new one. He'd arrived with the minimal amount of things. Only what he could pack in a moving pod. He didn't need the trappings of his old life; he was here to start fresh. A new place, a new job, possibly even a new fling?

A vision of Lilly smiling filled his mind. Bright green eyes dancing with humor, full red lips opening wide as a laugh escaped her at one of his corny jokes.

"Okay, just one more."

Lilly's lips curled into a wide grin as she shook her head. "How do you know so many pirate jokes?"

He shrugged. "My dad was the king of dad jokes, and pirate-themed ones were his favorite." And she kept laughing at them, which was making him feel like a god, so he'd keep telling them until he ran out.

With a slight nod, she picked up her glass, finishing off the drink she'd allowed him to buy her. "Okay, lay it on me."

Reaching into the recesses of his memory for his best one, he rubbed his hands together. "Okay, so a pirate walks into a bar with a steering wheel in his pants. The bartender says 'What's that doing there?' The pirate says—"

"Arrrrrr, it's drivin' me nuts."

His mouth dropped open in shock. "Holy cow, you're a

secret dorky-humor aficionado."

She laughed, the sound heating every inch of his body. When was the last time he'd had so much fun just talking with someone?

"No." She lifted one shoulder. "I just hang out with a bunch of firefighters from time to time, and they like jokes middle schoolers would tell."

"Hey," he protested but could tell she was just ribbing him from the gleam in her beautiful bright green eyes. Lincoln vowed then and there to tell all the bad jokes in his arsenal if it would make this woman laugh.

The woman had a great laugh. When he'd woken the next day to find her gone, he'd felt a slight pang of loss, wondering if he'd ever hear it again.

She might not want to sleep with him again, but they would be seeing each other frequently over the next month. Nothing said he couldn't try to make her laugh. He would swear the sun brightened when she did. Which was saying something, considering the only time he'd heard her laugh had been during nighttime.

They had amazing chemistry. Even the other day in her office, he'd felt the sparks fly. The shock of seeing her had only intensified, electrifying his entire system the closer he got to her. Sure, the fact that she denied knowing him had killed the buzz a little, but he understood her need for professionalism. She didn't date anyone in the wedding party. Okay, he could understand that in her line of work.

But I won't be in the wedding party forever.

By this time next month, Kenneth and Marie would be married, and that meant they would no longer be Lilly's clients, which also meant he would no longer be connected in any way to her job. Therefore, he had four weeks to get to know the woman and convince her to give him another shot. They didn't have to have a serious relationship or anything.

He wasn't too keen on doing that again any time soon. But nothing said they couldn't enjoy each other's company. Naked company. An entire month of mental foreplay.

A smile curved his lips. He might die getting there, but what a hell of a way to go.

Chapter Five

"Knock, knock, guess who?"

Lilly glanced up from the computer on her desk at the familiar sound of her third business partner, best friend, and former roommate. "Pru!"

Since Mo's desk was closer to the office door, the smaller woman got to their friend first, gently relieving Pru of one of the cuddly, cooing bundles she was carrying.

"Oh, thank you," Pru muttered as Lilly hurried over to take the other baby. "Finn dropped us off at the front. He didn't want the twins or me to walk too far in this weather."

It was pretty mild for January in Colorado. A small smattering of snow was left over from the last storm, but the sun shone brightly, and the temp was holding out at a mild fifty-two degrees. Practically flip-flop weather. But Pru's husband was the cautious type. Especially when it came to his wife and children.

A warm yearning panged in Lilly's heart. She could only imagine having a man as devoted and adoring as Finn. Her friend was lucky. Pru and Finn complemented each other in almost every way. They matched on paper and had amazing passion. Something like that only came around once in a great while. She was thrilled for her friend, truly, but a part of her ached for the pure and utter happiness she saw radiating off Pru since the woman had given her heart to the man she loved.

Lilly wanted that.

"I didn't think you were coming back to work until next week."

Simon giggled as she bounced him in her arms, the sweet baby boy staring at her, eyes wide with a toothless, slobbering grin.

"I'm not, but we got back from the hot springs yesterday, and I wanted to come in today to say hi. Plus, Finn wanted to check in at the station."

Pru's husband was one of Denver's finest firefighters. A tough job, but one he loved. With the demands of his job and the babies being almost seven months old, the couple had decided to take a short honeymoon close to home at the hot springs in Glenwood Springs. One thing the women always told a couple—even if it's only a few nights at a local hotel, take a honeymoon. Because it was the one thing that always seemed to get swept away for a future date that never came.

"How was the honeymoon?" Mo asked in between giving Sasha belly kisses, which delighted the baby girl, if her high-pitched giggles were anything to go by. "And don't leave out any naughty details."

"Leave out *all* the naughty details, please." Lilly shook her head at her roommate. "Get your kicks like a normal person and watch porn, Mo."

"Hey, I'm just trying to make sure my best friend's new husband is tending to her every need and I don't have to kick his ass."

Considering Mo was barely over five foot and maybe a

hundred pounds soaking wet, she doubted the woman could kick anything on the built firefighter.

"It was perfect." Pru smiled, taking a seat in one of the plush chairs facing Lilly's desk. "We soaked in the hot springs, went to dinner, got massages. I love the twins, but I'd forgotten how freeing it can be to do whatever you wanted whenever without having to worry about nap time or bringing extra clothes and diapers."

"Uh-huh." Lilly shared a knowing glance with Mo. "And how many times did you call Finn's parents to check in on the twins?"

Pru tugged at her ponytail, adjusting absolutely nothing, since the hairstyle was set perfectly. "Oh, not too often."

Mo snorted. "Only four times a day, then?"

Pru mumbled something under her breath.

"What was that? I couldn't hear over the delightful giggles of your children."

"Three, okay! I called them in the morning to check in, around lunchtime, and just before the babies' bedtime. And it wasn't only me freaking out; Finn insisted on video calls every night so he could read the twins their bedtime story."

Lilly exchanged a glance with Mo, chuckling when her friend started to laugh.

"We're only teasing you, sweetie," she said, adjusting Simon in her arms as the squirming baby made a grab for her glasses. "You and Finn are not only newlyweds but also new parents. Of course the first time leaving the twins would be hard."

Pru gave her and Mo a narrowed glare before a smile tugged at the corner of her mouth. "You two can be such bi— big doo-doo heads," Pru corrected, glancing at the twins.

"They're babies, Pru." Mo shook her head. "Pretty sure they're not going to understand swear words for another year or two."

"Which gives me that long to clean up my potty mouth. So, what have I missed this week? Anything exciting?"

Nervous sweat gathered on the back of Lilly's neck. She glanced to Mo, who graciously had her mouth shut, but her eyes were screaming warnings directly back at Lilly. Yeah, she had to tell Pru what happened. There might not be a real issue like there had been last time, but the women didn't keep secrets from one another. That's not what friends did. Especially when the information involved matters of business. That's not what business partners did.

"I slept with the best man."

Pru's jaw dropped. "What? Which best man?"

Kissing sweet Simon on his soft, soapy-smelling fuzzy ball of a head, she passed the baby off to his mommy and moved around her desk to take a seat. She couldn't tell this story while holding a baby. Her nerves were so jangled, she'd be afraid she might upset the poor thing. Mo also took a seat in the chair next to Pru, bouncing a giggling Sasha on her lap.

"I've got about half an hour before Finn gets back from the firehouse. Explain."

Taking a deep, calming breath—that in no way helped her calm down—Lilly dove right in.

"Okay, the night of your wedding was magical and beautiful, and everyone was ecstatically happy, including me," she rushed to say. "But I guess there was also a tiny part of me that was…"

"Horny?"

She glared at Mo. "Lonely."

The blond woman shrugged. "Same thing, sometimes."

Shaking her head, she continued explaining how she went to the bar for a drink, met Lincoln, and spent an amazing night with him. She glossed over the more intimate details—much to Mo's disappointment. Friends shared, but they didn't have to share *everything*. And she went on to say how she never thought she'd see the man again, until this week when he stepped into their office and she'd been introduced to the best man in Marie and Kenneth's wedding.

"And you have to believe me, Pru, I had no idea Lincoln had anything to do with their wedding or I never would have—"

"Sweetie, sweetie, stop." Rosy cheeks plumped as her friend smiled. "I know you had no idea. Mo and I trust you completely. What happened before wasn't your fault."

She scoffed. "Tell that to the lawsuit they filed."

"The lawsuit that failed."

"That's what I told her," Mo agreed.

It didn't matter what her friends said. She'd made a mistake once, and she didn't intend to do anything like that again. This was what she got for following her lust instead of logic. Oh God, she was as bad as her mother.

"No, you are not." Pru frowned. And Lilly realized she must have spoken that last thought out loud.

"Ooooh." Mo winced. "Speaking of your mother, she called us."

That couldn't be good. "Us? Us as in Mile High Happiness us?"

Mo and Pru exchanged a worried glance.

"Yeah, left a message saying for you to call her back."

The woman who gave her life could have called her cell phone. She knew Lilly's number. But her mother wouldn't because she didn't want to talk to Lilly her daughter. She wanted to talk to Lilly the wedding planner. How long had it been since her mother's most recent divorce? Almost a year, she figured. The memory of her last phone conversation with her mother played over in her mind.

"Franklin is such a deceitful bastard. I can't believe I ever married that louse!"

Far cry from the "Love God" her mother claimed him to

be when she married the guy. "I'm sorry, Mom. Maybe you should come out to Colorado and we can spend some time—"

"Oh baby, I'd love to, but Stavros is taking me away to Cabo for the weekend."

Of course her mother already had a new man. The ink from her previous divorce wasn't even dry yet.

"He's such a sweet guy. Not like those other jackasses who've pulled the wool over my eyes. Stavros is the real deal. A modern-day Prince Charming."

Lilly shook her head, clearing the memory. Same line different man, ever since she could remember. She had no doubt her mother would repeat the call in a few years, but this time Stavros would be the ass and her new man would be the great catch. Just another spin around the next man, the next wedding, the next future heartbreak carousel. Exhausting, but it was her mother. What could she do?

"I'll check our schedule and call her back later."

They'd helped plan the last two of her mother's weddings. She couldn't say why she kept doing it. The money? Sure, money helped pay for things like rent and food. Daughterly duty? Perhaps, but the sad fact of the matter was, Lilly suspected she allowed herself to be a part of her mother's ridiculous endless hunt for the perfect man because it was the only time her mother ever showed any interest in her child.

Sad? Yes, but if she wanted to spend time with her mother, it seemed someone had to get married, and since Lilly had zero prospects on that front, hello new stepfather.

"So." Pru smiled, trying to lighten the mood her mother's message had invoked. "Tell me more about Lincoln. Is he hot?"

"Sooooo freakin' hot!"

"Mo!"

"She asked."

"She asked *me*."

"Oh, like you were going to answer."

She hadn't intended to. Yes, the man was attractive, but he was off-limits now. No need to keep discussing him. That was like talking about your favorite ice cream when you were on a diet. Pointless and punishing.

"How do you even know what he looks like? You weren't here when he came in."

The small woman shrugged, kissing Sasha on her tiny button nose before answering. "I googled him."

"You did what? Why?"

"To make sure he wasn't another asshole. I knew you wouldn't check him out, so I did it for you."

That was sweet of her friend, she supposed. Slightly creepy, but sweet.

"Wanna know what I found out?"

"No!"

"Yes."

"Pru? Not you, too?"

The dark-haired woman shrugged. "Look, I'm not saying you should date the guy or engage in sexual activities with him again. In fact, you probably shouldn't, considering...well, everything. But aren't you just a little curious about him?"

No. She was perfectly happy with having one amazing night with Lincoln and never seeing him again. That was why she snuck out the morning after, but now...ugh! She couldn't sit here and listen to what Mo uncovered. It felt...wrong. Like stalking. Internet searching was something you did when you were interested in someone, and she was no longer interested in Lincoln Reid. Not one bit.

"According to all his social media accounts, he's single."

Okay, she was a little interested.

"He has a degree from the University of Nebraska in computer science. Works as a software developer, whatever the hell that is. He's in his early thirties, but I couldn't pinpoint a birthday."

And now it was getting creepy. She really couldn't do this. Standing, she grabbed her purse from her desk drawer and slung the strap over her shoulder.

"I'm going out for coffee. You two want anything?"

Mo glanced to their perfectly working coffee machine behind her desk, a knowing gleam filling her eyes, but she was smart enough to keep her mouth shut.

Pru tilted her head in confusion. "No, thanks. Finn will be back soon to pick me up."

"It was great seeing you. Enjoy the rest of your time off, and we'll see you next week, right?"

Pru nodded. Lilly took time to kiss each of the twins on their adorable little heads before heading out of the office and down the street. She had no idea where she was going—she didn't need coffee; they had an entire pot brewed no more than an hour ago. But after the message from her mom and the Lincoln stuff, the walls had started to close in. Her heartbeat had raced, and her throat swelled, making it hard to swallow. She needed air and a clear head.

She focused on the sound of her heels hitting the sidewalk, the feel of the chilly breeze against her skin. The slight stinging smell of cold in the air, signaling another impending snow.

Before too long, she got her body and mind calm once more. Lilly prided herself on keeping a cool head and solving any problem that came their clients' way, but often what you did for others was hardest to do for yourself.

Glancing around, she noticed she'd made it all the way to the Art District on Santa Fe just a few blocks away. And would you look at that, she was right in front of Marie and Kenneth's coffee shop, Déjà Brew. Perhaps she did need a cup after all.

She stepped inside the small coffee house, the warmth of

the air inside melting her chilled bones from the walk over and reminding her that, in her haste to leave the office without overhearing any more Lincoln knowledge, she'd grabbed her purse but forgotten her coat. Dummy.

A quick glance around revealed a tidy and cozy type of atmosphere. She'd never been to her clients' coffee shop. She liked it. The stack of classic board games in the corner and two shelves full of discounted used books gave the place a homey vibe. Not like those chain coffee shops where you came in for the latest trendy drink. This felt like a place a person could sit and enjoy a fine crafted beverage, maybe meet some friends for a game or stimulating conversation.

She made her way across the distressed hardwood floor to the counter, noticing the mishmash of tables, chairs, and cushioned seating filling the room. None of it matched, but that just made it feel more like someone's living room than a place of business. Kenneth and Marie were savvy. Make the customer feel like they're at home, and they'll come back time and again. No wonder the couple could afford Genesee Manor for their wedding.

"Hi, welcome to Déjà Brew. I'm Tristan. What can I get for you?"

She had just opened her mouth to order when a deep, familiar voice spoke from behind her.

"Whatever she wants is on the house, Tristan."

Whirling around, Lilly came face-to-face with the exact person who'd inadvertently driven her here in the first place. Lincoln Reid.

"What are you doing here? Where are Marie and Kenneth?"

He grinned—smug bastard—holding up a hand to explain.

"I'm here because Marie and Kenneth asked me to look after the shop. They're having lunch with her parents right now, and even though Tristan is a good worker, he's never manned the shop by himself before, so I'm here in case he needs any help."

"We're pretty quiet today, ma'am, but the fancy drinks take a little longer, and Mr. Reid offered to help if I get in a jam."

Did he just ma'am her? Oh God, the kid looked about seventeen, eighteen tops, but that only made him about a decade younger than her. Was she really ma'am-looking now?

"Just a coffee, please." She smiled at the young man. Not his fault he made her feel old; the kid was just being polite and a good employee. "Room for cream and sugar."

"We have a great fair-trade medium roast we just got in from—"

"That sounds perfect, thank you." She didn't need a big long spiel about where the beans came from. She just wanted to get her coffee and get out.

"No fancy coffee order?" Lincoln smiled. "Nothing with gobs of syrup and a dollop of whipped cream?"

She shook her head. "I prefer the simplicity of plain cream and sugar."

"Not me." His grin widened. "Give me all the sugary drinks, pumpkin spice, mocha latte, so sweet and full of vanilla. I need a sugar rush with my caffeine rush."

Ew, just thinking of a drink that sweet made her gag. She couldn't imagine the cavities this man must get from all that sugar. Who drank coffee that was basically a warm milkshake?

"So what brings you to the shop today?"

Lincoln stood at her side by the counter—far too close, in her opinion. Hadn't he ever heard of personal space? And the man could wipe that annoying grin off his face while he was at it. She was simply here to get coffee. No other reason.

"Just needed to grab a breath of fresh air and a cup of

coffee."

His grin widened. "Really?"

"Yes, really. Why else would you think I was here?"

He shrugged, the movement of his broad shoulders sparking memories of them bare and glistening with sweat as he moved above her, bringing her body to the peak of pleasure. She cleared her suddenly dry throat. Humor entered his hazel eyes, followed by a blaze of heat that nearly knocked her on her ass.

Dammit! He knew what she'd been thinking. Stupid, sexy jerk had probably been remembering the exact same moment. Too bad, bucko—they were a one-and-done type deal. She'd been under him, and now she was over him.

"I didn't come here looking for you."

His eyes widened in surprise. "I never thought you did."

Crap!

Maybe her subconscious had led her to Déjà Brew on the slim hope of finding Lincoln here. If she was going to learn more about the man, she wanted to hear it from the source, not her friends' internet search. Not that she did want to learn more about him. She absolutely did not.

Not at all.

"Well, um, good. So, are you enjoying your visit to Denver?" Okay, maybe she wanted to know a little bit about him. If she found out something distasteful, then she had a reason to not like him.

"It's great, but I'm not visiting."

"What?"

"Here's your coffee, ma'am."

Lilly ignored the barista as he set her to-go cup on the counter, Lincoln's words ringing in her ears, clanging out warning bells so loud they drowned out every other sound.

"What do you mean you're not visiting?"

He had to be visiting. The only facts she had on her

Lincoln-is-bad-on-paper list were that he was the best man in one of her weddings, he didn't do relationships, and he didn't live here. One issue would be resolved in a matter of weeks, and the others had to stick because he'd insinuated that he didn't do long-term. She did not want to fall for a guy who was just up for a fling, because Lilly knew herself. She didn't fling, she fell, and something told her falling for Lincoln Reed would be a very bad move.

"I live here now," he clarified. "Just moved into my place this week."

"Well that's just perfect!"

He chuckled. "Are you sure? Because you don't sound like it's perfect. You kind of sound like you want to throw your coffee on me. Please don't, by the way. I burn easily."

Oh, ha-ha, look at Mr. Sexy and Funny being all attractive and available and ruining the perfectly good wall she had in place for starting any kind of relationship with him.

But he doesn't do relationships.

Yes, she had to keep reminding herself of that very important fact.

Maybe I could just have a fling with him. A sexy, naked fling. I didn't fall after one night. What's the harm in a few more?

No she couldn't! Could she? No. Absolutely not.

"You... I...just... Ugh!" She was so frustrated she couldn't even think of a good comeback. Why was this man constantly throwing her off her game? She had to get out of here. Grabbing her coffee, she turned and headed toward the door.

"You forgot your cream and sugar," Lincoln called after her, laughter in his voice.

Resisting the urge to flip him off—he was still a member of her current wedding party—she waved a hand in the air, speaking around clenched teeth. "I've got some in the office.

Thanks."

His deep, infectious laughter followed her out the door and into the midday air, which had gotten even chillier in the ten minutes she'd been in the coffee shop. Even his laugh was sexy. Perfect. Now how was she supposed to resist him?

At least she still had the wedding. She could cling to that for the next few weeks. Who knows, maybe she'd discover he had a balloon fetish or liked banana cream pie. Banana wasn't a dessert, it was a fruit. She couldn't be with a man who considered fruit a dessert. *Oh please, please let Lincoln consider fruit a dessert.*

But a tiny part of her worried that nothing she could list or point to would make any difference. She'd had Lincoln once, and, though her mind knew it was a bad idea, her body craved another go-round.

She sighed. "I am so screwed."

Chapter Six

Two days later, Lilly and Mo stepped into The Gentleman's Finery, a suit and tuxedo shop on the edge of the Cherry Creek shopping area. The locally owned store was small but had excellent service and quality, and, keeping with her clients' wish to work with as many small business owners as possible, it fit the bill perfectly.

"Ms. Walsh, Ms. Rossi, how nice to see you again," Mr. Tanaka, the shop owner, called out.

The older gentleman made his way to her side. He reached out his wrinkled, talented tailor hands to grasp first hers and then her roommate's. The large, thick glasses magnified smiling eyes that never missed a single stitch despite the man's advanced age and worsening astigmatism. She knew from many years of conversations with the man at various client fittings that he took over the shop from his father, who took over from his father, who started the business after he immigrated to America from Japan in the early 1920s.

"Mr. Tanaka." Lilly smiled. "Always a pleasure."

"With you two beautiful and talented ladies in my shop,

the pleasure is always mine."

Old flirt. If he weren't thirty years older than her and madly in love with his wife of forty years, she'd snatch him right up. They fit perfectly on paper. Similar work fields, but not so similar as to cause marital issues; they both enjoyed the opera—she knew because he and his wife had given her their box tickets one night when they couldn't attend, best work perk ever—and they always had stimulating conversations. If only the Tanakas had a son. The couple did have two daughters. One who helped run the shop and the other who was away obtaining her PhD.

"I presume you're both here to oversee the Buller fitting?"

She nodded. "Yes. The gentlemen should be arriving any minute. Do you need us to help set anything up, or would we just be in your way?"

"You two could never be in my way." He motioned to the small collection of chairs and couches in the back of the shop. "Thank you for the offer, but I've got everything prepared. Why don't you both go sit and wait while I gather the gentlemen's tuxes?"

With that, the man hurried into the private back section of the store. Lilly followed Mo to the sitting area.

"When will the guys be here?"

She glanced at the time on her phone before answering her business partner. "Any minute now."

Mo sat in a plushy brown chair, her tiny frame sinking into the softness of the old, comfortable furniture. Lilly chose to seat herself on a firm, wooden high-back chair. Opening her planning binder, she flipped to today's section.

"We should have six men total. The father of the bride, father of the groom, ring bearer, the two groomsmen, and the groom."

"How old is the ring bearer?" Mo had her own binder sitting at her feet with all the answers she needed, but the woman's eyes were closed in bliss as she sank deeper into the chair.

What was that thing made of? Cotton candy?

Lilly scanned her notes. "He's six."

"Yes." Mo's pale brown eyes shot open. "Perfect age. Old enough to get the job done without crying down the aisle or throwing the ring pillow at the bride." Both of which they'd witnessed before. "But young enough not to be a punk ass."

Oh dear, she felt a headache coming on. Setting her binder in her lap, she removed her glasses, rubbing the bridge of her nose. "Moira, please, whatever you do, do not call the ring bearer a 'punk ass' in front of *any* member of the wedding party."

Mo laughed. "Oh, come on, like I would ever do anything like that. You worry too much, Lil."

She worried just the right amount, thank you very much. It was her roommate and business partner who didn't worry enough. Mo believed everyone was good—even punk-ass kids—and all would turn out right in the end no matter what. Her poor, delusional friend wouldn't believe she was going to drown even if someone strapped a cement block to her legs and pushed her into the Platte River.

"Just—" The chime above the shop door rang out. Lilly glanced over her shoulder to see Kenneth stepping in the front door, a group of men shuffling behind him. "Be nice."

Mo scrunched her nose in confusion. "I'm always nice."

True, but the woman had a snarky sense of humor not appreciated by everyone. It was why Lilly handled most of the customer-facing tasks while Pru handled the finances and Mo worked with vendors. But with a group this large, she needed backup.

Liar! You want Mo here so you don't jump Lincoln's fine bod again.

What the—? Where had that thought come from? It

certainly hadn't sounded like her. Sounded more like her sunny, snarky roommate. But the other woman had already stood and was stepping toward the approaching men with a huge smile on her face.

"Welcome to your tux fitting, gentlemen. I'm Moira Rossi, and this is Lilly Walsh, and we are two-thirds of Mile High Happiness. We can't wait to get you all looking devilishly handsome for Kenneth and Marie's big day."

Thankfully, her business partner had heeded Lilly's warning and turned on the charm. Every pair of eyes in the shop focused on Mo with rapt attention.

All but one.

Lilly glanced to the right of the groom to see Lincoln standing just behind Kenneth. His pale hazel eyes locked onto her with a singular focus that made shivers break out across her skin. A small smile tugged at the corner of his lips, eyes heating as she stared back, helpless to break the contact. He said something to Kenneth, and the groom nodded with a smile.

What was she doing?

Her client was here with his wedding party for a fitting she arranged—okay, Mo arranged it, but whatever—and here she sat, drooling like a dog over the hot best man.

Get a grip, Lilly, and do your job, not the groomsman.

Pasting a smile on her face, she rose from her seat and crossed over to the group.

"Kenneth, how are your nerves? Getting excited? Anxious? No cold feet?" She added a small laugh to the last part, but it was surprising how many people cracked when asked that question, even in jest. It helped save a doomed wedding a time or two. A handy tool in her arsenal in making sure their weddings went off without a hiccup.

The groom's smile widened, his entire face lighting up. "Are you kidding? I've been waiting for this day for years.

February can't come fast enough in my opinion. I just hope Marie doesn't come to her senses and realize she's too good for me before we say 'I do.'"

Lincoln nudged his friend with his shoulder. "That's what I've been saying for years, man. She's way too good for you."

"Ass," Kenneth muttered with a smile, shoving him back.

The rest of the men laughed along, commenting on the happy couple, the fathers of the bride and groom sharing sweet stories of when the two first called home about each other.

"They're actually quite perfect for each other."

Lilly started as the deep voice filled her ear. She glanced to her side to see Lincoln standing not a foot away. How the hell had he moved over to her side without her noticing? The man should wear a bell or something.

"Kenneth and Marie," he continued as she stared at him. "They've been through hell and come out stronger than ever."

"I know."

His brow raised. "You do?"

She nodded. "Marie told me about her…illness. It must have taken quite a toll."

"It did. On all of us." His smile slipped, gaze turning back to focus on his friend. "I'm not gonna lie, it sucked to know she was fighting so hard and there was nothing any of us could do. I thought poor Kenneth would need a new pair of feet with all the pacing he did in hospital waiting rooms."

The three were close. Best friends. She'd forgotten that Marie's cancer battle not only affected her fiancé but her friends as well. Poor Lincoln. She couldn't imagine what she would do if Mo or Pru ever got deathly ill. Watching Pru in labor had been bad enough.

Heart aching for him and the entire situation, she squeezed his hand gently. "But she's better now."

He glanced down to where her hand grasped his. His

eyes came up, fire blazing in the hazel depths. Suddenly her cheeks felt very hot, and sparks seemed to jump between their palms. She quickly dropped his hand and took a healthy step back.

No touching. Not anymore.

Lincoln smiled but didn't comment on her movement. He simply nodded.

"Yeah, she's better than ever, and those two are going to live the rest of their days in annoyingly mushy bliss."

She chuckled. "Yes, they are long-haulers."

He tilted his head, brow furrowing. "Long-haulers?"

"It's what we call them in the industry. A couple you just know is going to last, be together forever, the long haul. Don't get to see too many of them, but Kenneth and Marie are a pair. I can tell."

He stared at her, eyes narrowing. "Huh, interesting."

She swallowed, adverting her eyes, fearing she'd revealed too much.

"Welcome, gentlemen." Mr. Tanaka came out from the back, a rolling cart with a varying display of hanging tuxes on it. "I have a few selections based on the style and sizes requested. Shall we start with the little one?"

Lilly hadn't even noticed the small boy, who was clinging to the leg of the other groomsman, Marie's brother. The sweet little guy looked nervous as he stuck to his dad like glue.

"You can come too, Dad." Mr. Tanaka smiled. "We can fit you both at the same time."

Father and son followed the shop proprietor to the small dressing area in the back.

"Aren't wedding planners supposed to believe everyone lives happily ever after and all that stuff?"

She sucked in a sharp breath at the voice in her ear. How had he snuck up on her *again*? Turning, she glared.

"Will you stop sneaking up on me?"

Lincoln held out his hands, taking a very tiny step back. "Sorry. I didn't mean to sneak. I simply didn't feel like yelling my question from across the room."

"Three feet away is hardly across the room, Lincoln." He grinned, a very suspicious grin she did not like the look of. "What?"

"Nothing." He shrugged. "I just like it when you say my name."

Heat rose on her cheeks. Oh yes, she remembered well how much he liked it when she said his name. Liked it even better when she screamed his name as he drove her to the edge of— Nope! Time to stop that memory right now.

"Stop it," she whispered in a harsh tone.

"Stop what?"

"Flirting with me. It's inappropriate."

"As I recall…" He lowered his voice, forcing her to lean into him. "You like it when I get inappropriate."

Oh, for the love of— This man was going to drive her insane with frustration or lust or both.

"For your information," she said, "I do believe in happily ever after, I just don't believe everyone gets one."

His smile dropped. "You won't hear me arguing with you there."

Huh. She hadn't really expected him to agree with her. And that shift in mood… Her intuition was telling her Lincoln's lack of desire for a relationship had something to do with an unhappy breakup in his past. People often thought it was women who couldn't get over an ex, but in her experience, men had a much harder time letting go of past pain.

She brought her binder up to her chest like a shield. "In this business, you see a lot of people rushing into something for the wrong reason. A lot of people who think they want a marriage when all they really want is a big, fancy wedding."

"Nice payday for you no matter what."

That was a little cynical. "Yes, a payday is nice, but I want all my clients to be *happy*. When extenuating circumstance dictates, we've helped couples cancel their nuptials, sometimes at a loss to us. People shouldn't suffer just so others can make a living. Then there are the couples we have to hold our tongues around, the ones who go through with things even when they shouldn't. They think they know what they want even if everyone else can see the disaster ahead."

A dark pain filled his eyes, so sharp it took her breath away for a moment.

"Yeah, I guess some people just can't see the truth sometimes."

No, they couldn't. A very true statement, and one that spoke of past experience, perhaps? A painful one, if she were a betting woman. Which she was not.

"So." He shook his head, the dark expression dissipating. "You're pretty good at spotting the disasters?"

For everyone else? Yes. For herself? Not a chance.

"It's my job," she answered with a smile.

"Hmm."

He nodded, his eyes searching hers, seeking out truths she was in no way ever going to reveal to him.

Not a chance, buddy. We were one and done. Body-baring only. No soul reveals for you.

"My personal life is another matter."

Dammit, brain! What did I just say?

How did this man throw her so off-kilter? Did he have a magic penis that cast a confusion spell on her when they had sex or something?

"Really?" He chuckled. "Do tell."

Not for a million dollars.

Adjusting her glasses, she stepped back. "Excuse me, Mr. Reid, but I have some important wedding issues I need to discuss with the groom. I'm sure Mr. Tanaka will be ready to start your tux fitting soon."

With what she hoped passed for a polite smile, she turned and hightailed it over to Kenneth, who was speaking with Mo about the wedding colors.

"Marie wanted our fathers' vests to be a different color than the groomsmen's," Kenneth said as she approached.

"We can do that," Mo agreed. "Did you two have a specific color in mind?"

The groom shrugged. "Whatever goes with green and lavender."

Lilly stepped to his side. "How about silver? It's subtle enough not to overpower the primary colors and will give a classic, regal feel to the patriarchs of your families."

Kenneth smiled. "Yeah, silver. It's perfect. Man, I am so glad we hired you, Lilly. I wish you could manage the coffee shop, too."

She gave a soft laugh. "I probably wouldn't be as effective at solving coffee crises."

He laughed with her before being called over by Mr. Tanaka to approve the first of the selected tuxes. Lincoln had taken up a conversation with the fathers, leaving Mo and Lilly in relative isolation.

"You and Lincoln looked pretty chummy over there." Mo waggled her eyebrows. "What were you talking about?"

"Wedding stuff."

"Really? Is that what the kids are calling it these days?"

She sighed. "That doesn't even make sense, Mo."

"It does if you have a sense of humor."

Crass, but not entirely untrue. There may have been a past boyfriend or two who accused Lilly of being a stick-in-the-mud. Excuse her for taking life as seriously as it was. Besides, she knew how to have fun. She had a sense of humor. It was just hard for her to let her hair down. She had a business to run.

"Hey," Mo said softly, placing a hand on Lilly's arm. "Seriously, is everything okay?"

She glanced over to Lincoln, who, thankfully, was fully engaged in his conversation and not paying them any attention. Just in case, she turned so her back faced the men, blocking her and Mo's discussion. Glancing into her friend's worried gaze, she let out a breath and the truth along with it.

"I'm just a little stressed out with Pru still gone and my mother calling."

Okay, partial truth.

"Oh sweetie, why didn't you say anything?" Mo pulled her in for a quick hug. "Let's take a break tonight and do something fun."

"The only thing I want to do tonight is Lincoln." She slapped a hand over her mouth, eyes widening. "Laundry," she hissed at her friend's surprised expression. "I meant the only thing I want to do tonight is *laundry*. I have a huge pile of colors to run."

"Nice try, but I heard the Freudian slip."

"Mo." She glanced over her shoulder, but all the men were still occupied. "Please."

The shorter woman sighed. "Fine. We won't discuss your pathetic lusting over a guy you already had and could have again if you just let go of your silly self-imposed rule, but I am not letting you wallow in dirty laundry tonight. There's only one thing to do with pent-up lust you can't sate."

"What?" She eyed her roommate warily; nothing Mo suggested could be good. She loved her friend, but she didn't exactly trust her.

Mo gave a sneaky little grin, winking as she replied, "Smack some balls, of course."

Chapter Seven

Lincoln let his gaze travel over the crowded barcade. This place was awesome. When Marie and Kenneth had suggested getting out tonight to show him some of the city's highlights, he expected they'd go to some hipster bar, knowing his friends' taste. But he hadn't expected to find an establishment that combined two of his favorite things: beer and arcade games. Even if it was a little hipstery.

Where he lived in Nebraska, they had bars, sure, but they were your standard-type watering holes: booze, table and chairs, dartboard on the wall, maybe a jukebox in the corner. Not a one of them had this—a wall of pinball machines that made Lincoln's fingers itch with the need to slide a shiny silver quarter in the slot and take out all his stress by whacking a tiny metal ball over and over.

The bells and whistles of the various games ringing out winning and losing chimes made his lips curve in a grin.

"Told you he'd like it, babe," Kenneth said from behind him.

Marie squeezed his arm. "Why don't we grab a drink?

Then you can go hog wild, Mr. Pinball Wizard."

He chuckled at the nickname he'd been given in college. He was known around campus to relieve the stress of finals week by challenging anyone in the student lounge to a pinball competition. And winning. Lincoln wasn't one to brag, but, okay, yeah, he'd brag about his pinball skills, because they were awesome.

They made their way up to the bar, pushing through the crowd to finally find a spot. Kenneth nodded to the bartender, who seemed to recognize him. In less than ten minutes, he and Kenneth had a couple of beers while Marie had a Shirley Temple.

Lincoln took a long pull from his stout, following Kenneth and Marie away from the crowded bar and to a small table near the back. From here, he could see the entire room. The lighting was dim, as with most bars, but the bright, flashing lights of the various arcade games lit up the place with bright yellows, blues, and reds. As he glanced around the room, his eyes fell on a familiar face.

He leaned over to speak loudly in his friends' ears over the din: "Is that Mo and Lilly?"

He pointed to the side wall, which housed all the pinball machines, where two women stood, one short with blond hair streaked with blue and one tall with silky dark brown hair falling down her back, eyes focused on the game in front of her as she racked up the points on the scoreboard in a fairly impressive number.

Lilly Walsh was a pinball player? Damned if the woman didn't get more and more enticing with each thing he learned about her.

"What?" Kenneth squinted to see where Lincoln was pointing. "Oh, yeah, that's them. Mo loves this place. In fact, we found out about their wedding planning business because they're friends with Kip, the bartender."

"Ooooh, giant Jenga just freed up!" Marie exclaimed. "Lincoln, go see if Mo and Lilly want to join us for a game."

A grin tilted his lips. "You got it, Marie."

He stood, making his way through the throng of people. As he approached the women, their backs to him, both focusing on the ball, he watched as Lilly finessed the game with a skill that rivaled his own.

The woman was good. The thought made him smile. His ex hated his obsession with arcade games. Jessa always said they were immature; she'd never be caught dead playing anything beyond rummy or solitaire. Sophisticated adult games.

Whatever the hell that meant. What made a deck of cards more sophisticated than a complex arcade machine?

Lilly growled in frustration, slamming her hand against the glass top of the pinball machine. "Dammit! I was only a thousand points away from a high score."

Clearing his throat, he stepped closer so as to be heard above the pinging of the machines.

"Impressive score, Ms. Walsh."

Lilly and Mo turned as one to face him, a very different expression on each woman's face. They both appeared surprised to see him there, but Mo's face morphed into happy excitement while Lilly's eyes widened right before she scowled at him.

"Seriously?" She threw her hands up in the air, frustration clearly etched on every beautiful inch of her face.

"Sorry." He grinned. "Were you expecting someone else?"

"I was expecting to play my game in peace, without being interrupted by the reason…"

"The reason for what?" He tilted his head, curious why his presence here seemed to bother her so much.

"Yeah," Mo said, a cheeky grin on her face. "By the

reason for what exactly, Lil?"

He watched in fascination as the two women seemed to have an entire conversation with nothing more than their eyes. There might have been some lowly muttered words, but the place was really loud and Lincoln couldn't pick anything up. Though he thought he caught Mo say the word "relax."

Lilly sighed, pasting on a ridiculously fake smile and turning to him. "What brings you to 1up tonight?"

He smiled, in no way fooled by her false sense of cheer.

"Kenneth and Marie wanted to show me some of their favorite spots in the city." He turned slightly, pointing back and to the left. "They're over there playing giant Jenga. Marie wanted to know if you two would like to join us for a game."

Mo hopped up and down. "Ooooh, I love giant Jenga. Count me in!"

"Uh, Mo, don't you think—?"

But Mo ran off before Lilly could finish, tossing Lincoln a wink over her shoulder as she left.

He liked Mo, but not as much as he liked the woman standing in front of him with a frustrated little frown pulling at her lips.

"You in?"

She bit her lip. A lip he vividly remembered nibbling on himself. His body tightened with need, every muscle tensing with anticipation. *Calm down, man.* The woman made it pretty clear she didn't want to get in bed with him again. Actually, she made it clear they *shouldn't* go to bed together again. Judging by the heated look in her eyes, what she wanted and what she'd allow herself were two very different things.

But he would never push her into anything she might regret later, so he motioned to the machine behind her.

"Or we could play this?"

At that, her eyes widened in surprise. "You play pinball?"

He snorted. "No. Other people play pinball. I *dominate*

pinball."

A disbelieving laugh escaped her lips. "Really? Wanna bet?"

"Depends on what we're betting for." He bobbed his eyebrows in an overly comical manner.

Lilly laughed, shaking her head. "How about bragging rights?"

Not what his first choice would be, but he got her to laugh again, so he'd call it a win and agreed, motioning to the pinball machine with a wave of his hand. "Ladies first."

Lilly grabbed another quarter from her pocket and put it in the machine, starting a new game.

Lincoln watched, enthralled with the skill she used to coax the ball exactly where she wanted it to go. Her fingers deftly worked the flipper buttons to send the ball flying up the ramps to fall back down and hit every single sensor on the game, sending her score sailing into the high hundreds of thousands.

He whistled. "Not bad. You're good."

"Thanks," she said, focus never leaving the game. "And don't try to distract me with any of your corny pirate jokes."

He grinned, unable to resist the gauntlet she'd just thrown down. "Don't worry about that. I've traded in my pirate jokes for more meaningful pursuits. As a matter of fact, right now I'm reading a fascinating book about gravity." He paused for dramatic effect before leaning in close and saying, "It's impossible to put down."

Lilly bent over the machine, laughter bursting out of her, the last silver ball rolling down the ramp past her flippers, ending her turn. Turning to face him, she took a moment to control herself, but her lips were curved in a wide, beautiful smile as she pointed a finger at him accusingly.

"You cheated."

"Hey." He held up his hands in surrender. "Technically it

wasn't a pirate joke."

Rolling her eyes, she gave him a tiny shove. "Your turn, funny man."

Lincoln stepped up to the game, fishing a quarter out of his pocket and sliding it into the coin slot. He worked the machine, following the ball with a keen eye, fingers light and ready on the flapper buttons. It took him his first two balls and a couple thousand in score to get the feel of the game, but once he did, Lincoln was in the zone.

"Impressive, Mr. Reid."

Lilly's softly whispered words in his ear sent a shiver up his spine, hardening a part of his anatomy thankfully hidden by the large metal gaming equipment in front of him.

"Now who's cheating?" he tossed over his shoulder. Honestly, he didn't mind her method of distraction. If he thought for one minute her little breathy come-on was real, he'd tank this game so fast—but as much as he wished, he knew Lilly still had an issue with picking up where they left off. So he kept his attention on the game, 100 percent.

The warm feel of her arm pressed against him as she leaned over his shoulder to watch him play...

Okay, 75 percent.

After ten excruciating minutes trying to concentrate on the game while the woman he wanted more than his next breath did her best to distract him simply by existing, he glanced up at his score. Not his highest by any means, but a solid ten thousand over Lilly's. He figured that was good enough and let his final ball sink.

"Dang," Lilly muttered as he turned to face her. "You are good."

"Yeah, I didn't have a lot of friends in middle school, but we did have a pinball machine in the basement of our house. Spent a lot of time with that thing." It was his safe place, that pinball machine.

A sad light entered her eyes as she stared at him. "You didn't have friends?"

He shrugged, uncomfortable with the sympathy in her gaze. He didn't need it. Yeah, maybe he'd been a lonely kid growing up, but he had Kenneth and Marie now. "I was an übernerd. Really into computers and gaming. All the other kids were into sports and stuff. Not really my scene. How about you?"

She scrunched her nose, pushing her glasses up with a finger when they slipped down. "I was my high school's varsity volleyball captain two years in a row. I can't say I'm into gaming other than pinball."

He chuckled, in no way surprised that the slightly uptight Lilly wasn't a gamer. "Are you telling me you don't play *D&D*? *Pathfinder*? *The Settlers of Catan*? *Small World*? *Smash Up*? You never had LAN parties with computer geeks as a kid?"

Her head tilted as she gave him a droll stare. "I have no idea what any of those things are, but no, none of them really sound up my alley."

"At least we have pinball." He gave her a wink. "Wanna play again?" He motioned to the game.

She shook her head. "No way can I beat that score."

He smiled. "I told you it was my game."

"True, but aren't you supposed to let your date win?"

His eyes widened, hopeful warmth radiating through his chest. "Is this a date?"

"What? No!" Panic erased all the joy from her face as she glanced over at Mo, who stood laughing with Kenneth and Marie as the giant wooden blocks wobbled in the wonky tower on the table between them. Damn, he hadn't meant to make her feel uncomfortable.

"I was kidding, Lilly." Kind of. Sort of. Not really, but if it made her feel better, he could pretend.

A sad, wistful glint entered her eyes. "I didn't mean... We can't... I don't date clients. I told you that."

She had, but he did feel the need to remind her, "You did, and I told you I'm not your client."

"But I also said I don't date members of the wedding party. It's just...it's not good for business."

Hmm, the way she said that... He wondered if there was a story behind her decision. No. He didn't wonder that. He shouldn't, because the more he learned about Lilly Walsh, the more he liked her. And lusting after her was fine, but liking her? That could fall into dangerous relationship territory, and Lincoln did not want to risk that heartache. Not again.

Having fun was one thing. Caring was quite another.

Lilly turned her head back to their friends. "Maybe we should go check in with the others?"

Yeah, that might be for the best. He liked hanging out with Lilly, and that could turn into a problem. If they weren't on the same page about what they wanted? Well, that was a recipe for disaster, and no way would he do anything to negatively impact Kenneth and Marie's special day.

He smiled, stepping back to give her and himself plenty of room. Touching her again was a bad idea right now. So instead he grabbed his drink from the side table where he set it before his game and motioned for her to lead the way. "Sure. Let's go."

As they turned, someone jostled her from behind. She stumbled, and Lincoln reached out, catching her arm before she fell but not before she spilled half her drink all over her shirt.

"Dammit!" She pulled the wet, sticky material away from her chest.

"You okay?" Anger burned in his gut as he glanced over the crowd for whoever bumped her. He knew the place was crowded and a lot of people were a few drinks in, but damn, people needed to be more careful.

"I'm fine. It was an accident."

"Do you want another drink?"

She shook her head, a sigh falling from her lips. "No. But I wish I had a dry shirt."

Without saying a word, he set down his beer and peeled his long-sleeved sweater up and over his head, handing her the dark blue garment.

"Do you have to be chivalrous *and* sexy?" she groused, snatching up the offered sweater.

He let out a soft, confused laugh. "Sorry?"

"I don't believe that for a second. Go." She motioned to where the others stood playing giant Jenga. "I'm going to change, and then I'll meet you."

He nodded, making his way over to the table but keeping an eye on her as she entered the bathroom. Lilly Walsh was a conundrum he couldn't figure out. Probably best for him if he didn't, but damned if he wanted to anyway.

Chapter Eight

"Shit, shit, shit!" Lilly pounded the keys on the office computer, yielding zero results.

"What is it?" Pru asked.

The third member of Mile High Happiness had come back from her time off for her honeymoon just this morning, all glowing and happy and sexually satisfied and adding to the mounting frustration threatening to make Lilly explode. Not fair. It wasn't her friend's fault she found the best guy in the world and was now living happily ever after in wedded and parental bliss. Just because Lilly was currently suffering a case of horny-for-a-man-she-couldn't-have didn't mean she got to be all surly about her friend's happiness.

That wasn't what good friends did.

"This stupid computer froze again," she complained, smacking her hand against the side of the flat screen.

"Did you try control-alt-delete?" Mo asked from her desk along the far wall.

"Yes, Moira. It didn't do anything."

"Turning it off and turning it back on again?" her

roommate suggested.

A low, frustrated growl escaped her lips. "I tried, but it won't turn off. The damn thing is frozen, and nothing I do is helping."

Mo shrugged. "Well, that's all I got, sorry."

Lilly hit the escape button. Nothing. She moved the mouse around on the thick pad with their logo on it. Still nothing. The damn thing didn't even move on the screen. It stood still. Frozen. Not responding no matter what she did.

"Ahhhh!" She let out an irritated scream. "I hate computers!"

She and technology did not get along. A discredit to her generation, she'd never understood much more than basic programs like Word and Excel. Give her a good old-fashioned pen and paper and she could run the world. Or her world, at the very least. But tell her to put all her carefully laid plans into an operating system, and Lilly was a goner.

"Why does the world have to run on computers?"

"Because it's the twenty-first century." Mo chuckled. "Luddite."

True. And she did love the convenience of certain technologies: her cell phone, streaming services, the internet. But for some reason, computers—this one in particular—had a grudge against her. It taunted her daily. Freezing on her, locking up, losing important documents she knew she saved. One of the reasons she insisted they keep paper files and receipts in addition to having an online system. She didn't trust this damn computer one bit. It was out to get her.

"Want me to call our tech guy?" Pru asked, reaching for her phone.

Lilly shook her head. "No. He's out of town this week. Some conference or something." Figures her computer would break down the exact moment their IT connection was out of reach.

"Oh, dang. Should we call a service or take it to a shop or something?"

"Let me make some calls." Lilly sighed, but after half an hour on the phone to every computer repair service/shop/tech geek listed online, Lilly's mood had gone from frustration to despair.

"Crap!" She slammed down the office phone.

"What?" Pru asked.

Adjusting her glasses on her nose, Lilly glared at the stupid, broken hunk of technology in front of her. "I've called every place I can find, and no one has any availability until the end of the week."

"Lil," Mo said from her desk across the room. "I know you have paper files of everything and all, but we can't go the rest of the week without a computer. It'll create some serious issues. We should just replace the thing."

They should, but even a new computer wouldn't help their current situation.

"We need a plan C." She racked her brain, poring through all the possibilities to try and find a solution to the problem. That was her thing. Solutions. A point of pride in herself had always been her ability to find another answer, so why was her brain failing her at the moment?

"I have an idea," Mo piped up cheerfully.

Dang, how had her roommate, who flew through life on a spur-of-the-moment-type attitude, come up with a solution before her? Maybe she hadn't had enough coffee this morning. Brain fog due to lack of caffeine. She had been having difficulty sleeping the past few nights. She was just stressed.

No. You're horny and lusting after a man you can't have.

Harsh but true. Her past few sleepless nights could be directly blamed on a certain sexy best man and the unexplainable pull he had on her. What was it about Lincoln

Reid that made her body ache and crave? She'd already had the man. He should be out of her system. Yet every time she saw him, her desire to rip his clothes off and have her wicked way with him again ramped up even more.

"We know a guy who works with computers who would probably help us out for next to nothing," Mo pointed out.

Pru tilted her head, brow wrinkling. "We do?"

What? The only other computer guy they knew was—

Oh hell no!

"No." She shook her head, refusing to see this as a possible solution. There had to be something else, some*one* else.

Mo grinned, an evil glint filling her eyes. "Yes."

Pru glanced back and forth between the two of them. "I'm missing something."

"We're not calling Lincoln."

"Why not? He's a tech guy. I'm sure he can fix our computer in five seconds."

"Wait." Pru held up a hand, a slight grimace on her face. "Lincoln as in sexy best man Lincoln who Lilly has a thing for?"

"I do not have a thing for him!"

"The lady doth protest too much, methinks," Mo said in a mock hushed tone to Pru.

"We don't even have his number." See? Lincoln couldn't be the solution to their problem if they had no way to contact him.

"Yes we do." Mo flipped through the mess on her desk until she came up with a small slip of paper. "Marie gave it to me in case of emergency."

Well crap.

"What's wrong?" Her roommate waved the tiny paper in the air. "Chicken?"

Reluctant to admit it but knowing there was no other

solution, Lilly rose from her desk and marched over to Mo. Snatching the paper from her friend's hand, she pointed.

"I'm only using this to get him to fix our computer."

Mo held up her hands. "Whatever you say. But you better put the number in your contacts just in case. Ya know, for any *emergency* that might come up."

Only Mo could make an innocuous word like "emergency" sound like sex. Her friend had a talent—an evil talent, but a talent nonetheless.

"Mo." Pru shook her head slightly. "Lil is using her brain about this whole…situation. Give her a break, will ya?"

At least one of her friends was on her side.

Heading back over to her desk, she pulled out her cell phone, staring at the ten tiny numbers in stark black ink on the bright white piece of paper in her fingers. She really had no choice. It wasn't about her needing him; this was about the business needing his specialized set of skills.

And boy does the man have skills.

She told her horny self to shut up. This was about computers, not bedrooms.

Taking a deep breath, she dialed the number and reminded herself she was a professional with strict rules set in place for a reason. This was a business call, not a booty call.

• • •

Lincoln stared at his phone, debating whether or not to answer. Usually he ignored numbers he wasn't familiar with. If it was important, the person would leave a message and he'd get back to them, but it was usually just a telemarketer.

The phone rang for a third time, and he almost let it go to voicemail, but something in him kicked. He had no idea why, but he had the strongest urge to pick up the phone and answer. So he did.

"Hello?"

"Lincoln?"

He paused, sure his ears were deceiving him. "Lilly?"

"Yes, um, hi."

Must be his lucky day. Lilly Walsh was calling him. How did she get his number? Probably from Marie. She'd asked him if she could give it to the wedding planners in case of emergency, and he'd agreed. But what the hell kind of emergency could Lilly have that needed his assistance?

Oh, please let it be the naked kind.

Wishful thinking.

"So, um, I understand you do computer stuff."

If she meant applying mathematical analysis and computer science principles in order to develop software for companies to use, then yeah. He did *computer stuff.*

"Need a company computer guy?"

His new job didn't start until after the wedding. He'd decided to take a few weeks off in between to help Kenneth and Marie and also get a feel for his new city, but honestly, he had been getting bored. His friends didn't need as much help as they thought, and Lincoln didn't do great with idle time. He had his entire apartment unpacked within the first few days, and there was only so much exploring he could do before he got antsy. He needed to code, tinker, fix something, or have wild hot sex with a beautiful, poised wedding planner. Since that last one was off the table—for now—he'd go with the first option.

"That's the thing." Lilly's voice carried over the phone. "My computer froze, and nothing I do is working to fix it. The person who normally fixes our computer problems is out of town, and—"

"Say no more. I'll be over in ten."

"Are you sure?" Uncertainty rang in her voice, along with something else…edginess. "I wouldn't want to pull you away from any important work."

"You're not." He'd been installing a new Linux distro on his home server and trying to figure out the driver for his GPU. Nothing he couldn't attend to later.

"Thank you."

He hung up, a huge smile tugging at his lips. She hadn't wanted to call him; that was clear from her tone. But something else had been clear, too. She needed him, and not just for the computer problem. He'd heard the breathiness of her voice, the subtle longing when she said his name. He recognized it because it was the exact same need that colored his voice every time he talked about the woman. She may not want to want him, but she did.

That was something, at least.

Heading out of his apartment, he hopped into his car and drove toward Mile High Happiness, grateful Marie suggested putting the address in his GPS "just in case." The streets of Denver were a maze of one-way confusion. In the short amount of time he'd been living here, he'd almost driven down the wrong street four times. Who the hell designed this city?

He pulled into the building's lot a few minutes later. The large, twenty-story building had office space on the first level and apartments above, so the parking lot was filled with mostly resident parking spots, but there were a few visitor spots up front, and he was lucky enough to grab one. Another thing he'd learned about Denver since moving here—the city had crappy parking options. But other than the weird streets and limited parking, he loved it. So far everyone had been really friendly, the restaurant options were diverse and delicious, and the mountains in the distance were breathtaking. He could see why so many people moved to Denver.

Locking his car, he headed straight to Mile High Happiness. He opened the glass door with the etched frosted flowers and saw three women huddled around a computer: Mo, a woman he didn't recognize, and, sitting right in the middle, the woman who starred in every single one of his recent dreams: Lilly Walsh.

"Did you try this button?"

"Yes, Moira." Lilly shook her head, a frown marring her beautiful face. "I tried every damn button on this thing. It's broken, okay?"

Since none of the women realized he'd come in the door, he cleared his throat. "Mind if I take a look?" That was why she'd called, after all.

Three heads popped up with varying expressions filling their faces. Mo broke out into a bright, welcoming smile. The woman he didn't know tilted her head to study him with a smaller, uncertain smile. Lilly glared at the computer in front of her, but when she spotted him, he swore he saw a bit of relief filling those beautiful eyes. As much as he wished that happy gaze was for him, he'd bet his last bit of RAM it was for his tech skills.

"Lincoln." Mo hurried from behind the desk to greet him. "Thank you so much for coming. Another few minutes and I think Lilly would have hurled the computer into the wall."

"Don't put it past me yet," the seated woman muttered.

He laughed softly. "Before you ruin your lease by damaging property walls, let's see if I can be of help."

He stepped around the desk to Lilly's free side. The woman standing beside Lilly held out her hand.

"Hi, I'm Pru. The third member of Mile High Happiness. And you must be Lincoln, the...*best* man."

"Prudence," Lilly growled under her breath.

He shook the woman's hand, wondering at her emphasis. How much did Lilly's partners know about what happened between them?

"Thank you for coming. Now, can you just fix this damn thing before it gives me a stroke?" Lilly pushed back from the desk, rising from her seat and motioning for him to occupy it.

"I'll do what I can." It would probably be an easy fix. Most computer issues were operator error. He'd bet it would take no time to sort out whatever the problem was.

"Hey, I have an idea," Mo said a bit too cheerfully. "Why don't Pru and I go grab everyone dinner while you and Lincoln fix whatever issue this is?"

Why did he hear something other than *computer issue* in that offer?

"We don't need dinner right—"

Mo cut Lilly off. "Yes, we do. I'm hungry, and I know Pru is, too."

"I am?" the other woman asked with a raised brow.

"Yes, you are. Besides, we need to show Lincoln we appreciate his help somehow."

Lilly narrowed her eyes at her friends. "We can pay him."

"Dinner sounds like a perfect payment to me," he chimed in with a grin.

She sent a death glare his way, but he was having too much fun to be intimidated by it.

"Perfect, then we'll just head out and let you two figure this out." Mo grabbed Pru by the arm and practically dragged the other woman out of the office despite her soft protest. "Bye!"

The moment they left, he released the laughter he'd been holding in. "She's not subtle, is she?"

"About as subtle as a Mack truck," Lilly grumbled.

He tapped away at the keys, but the screen remained frozen. "So, I can assume the no-sex-with-wedding-party-members is a personal rule and not a company-wide policy?"

"You can assume whatever you like." Her haughty voice sounded in his ear as she leaned in close to see what he was doing. "You know what they say about assuming."

Yes. He was familiar with the saying.

After trying a few more key combinations, he realized that whatever happened to this computer, it needed a hard reboot. Nothing else would bring it back from the frozen screen of death. He held down the power button, noticing the main reason it might be malfunctioning was because it had to be a solid ten years old. A dinosaur, in computer terms. His fitness tracker probably had more RAM than this thing.

Once the computer started back up, he went into the system console and scanned for any new errors, happy to see there were none.

"There. All done."

"You fixed it?"

"I fixed it, but you might want to think about upgrading to a newer computer soon."

Lilly leaned over him, staring at the screen as if it held the answers to life.

"Just like that? You came in here and solved my problem with a few clicks of the keyboard?"

Not quite so simple, but basically. He'd figured it'd be a fairly easy fix; what he couldn't understand was why she seemed upset by it.

"Yup. Happy to help."

With a huff, she pushed herself up and started to pace back and forth from the wall to the desk, frustration fueling her every step.

"Of course you're happy to help. You're always happy to help. You're just one helpful, happy guy."

"Um, did I miss something?"

She ignored him, continuing to pace.

"You can't even have the decency to be an asshole or have a bad habit. No, you're just so damn helpful and sweet and sexy."

That got him to smile. "You think I'm sexy?"

He kind of figured she didn't find him hideous, since she had slept with him. But it never hurt a guy's ego to hear an insanely beautiful woman found him attractive. He rose from the chair, risking life and limb—or at least the very real possibility of a knee to the nuts—by moving into her pacing path. She didn't slow down, didn't even notice he moved, merely crashed into him. He reached out to grab her arms, steadying her when she would have tumbled.

"Ugh! You even smell good. This isn't fair, Lincoln. You're impossible to resist."

His brow rose as it dawned on him that her anger stemmed from sexual frustration. And he was the source of it. That went a small way to easing his bruised pride from waking up the morning after their amazing night together to find her gone.

"Really?" His gaze roamed over her face, pausing on her lips. Lips he tasted once, lips he tasted every night in his dreams, lips he burned to taste again. "You seem to be doing a pretty good job of resisting me so far."

Her hands came up—to push him away, he'd bet—but he bet wrong. Lilly grabbed two fistfuls of his shirt. With a frustrated moan, she tugged, pulling him down as she lifted her chin. Her mouth crashed against his, those sweet lips colliding with his own, tasting even better than he remembered.

Surprise kept him immobile for all of 0.1 seconds before he came to life, tugging her by the grip he had on her arms, pulling her into him until he could feel every inch of her soft, heavenly body pressed against his.

Yes! This was what he'd been missing, been craving. This passionate, fiery woman who knew what she wanted and took it. This was the Lilly he met that night at the hotel. The one who brought him to his knees. He'd known she was there, hiding under all that prim and properness. Though he had to admit, the prim and proper thing was hot as hell too. Seemed no matter what this woman did or how she acted, it never ceased to get his motor running.

She moaned, low and deep, the sound causing him to harden to the point of pain. She backed them up, lips still fused as if their lives depended on it, until he felt his back hit the hard, solid wall. He didn't care. She could bash his head against all the walls she wanted as long as she kept kissing him. Because kissing Lilly was the best damn feeling he'd ever experienced.

Second best.

Being inside her held the honor of the first.

"Dammit!"

Her muttered curse reached him through a fog of lust. One second she had her tongue halfway down his throat, and the next she was gone. Pulled out of his embrace and standing a foot away. Felt like a million miles to him.

"Lilly?" Her name came out shaky, because he was feeling damn shaky. The woman had that effect on him.

Her dark hair was mussed, clothing wrinkled, glasses slightly askew on her sharp nose. She adjusted her frames with a single finger, then pointed that finger at him.

"That did not happen."

"Okay..." But it had.

Any further discussion was halted by her friends coming back, arms filled with bags.

"We got burritos from— Hey!" Mo stared in confusion as Lilly hurried past her. "Where are you going? We have food."

Lilly stopped, her gaze swinging back to him. "I'm not hungry for food."

She was hungry for him and not happy about it. He read that clearly in her gaze.

"I need some air." And with that, she stormed out the office door and was gone.

"Okay." Pru headed to the back desk, setting her bag on it and taking food containers out. "That was weird."

You could say that again.

Mo made her way to Lilly's desk, giving him a soft smile. "You'll have to be patient with her. She's not used to being attracted to a guy she considers off-limits. It's kind of messing with her head."

Fair enough—*she* was messing with *his* head.

"But, Lincoln?"

He tore his gaze away from the door where Lilly had stormed out and focused on her friend. Mo's smile slipped, a deadly calm entering her honey brown eyes.

"If you hurt her, I'm going to make you a special batch of my nonna's laxative brownies. Got it?"

He nodded. He got that—solidarity in friendship and all—but her friend had him and Lilly all wrong. They were about the physical connection, not an emotional one. Right? He thought he'd been pretty open with Lilly about what he could give to a woman, but maybe he should clear the air again. Maybe she was resisting so much because she thought he wanted more of a commitment—which he sure as hell did not—and worried what would happen when everything went south.

Nothing would go south, because Lincoln didn't want more than another night or two, or twenty, in Lilly's bed. She wanted the same, right? His stomach tensed. Maybe he should take a step back from all this until he and Lilly had a real talk about what they wanted. Of course, that would mean the woman would have to sit down and actually have a conversation with him without either biting his head off or kissing the daylights out of him.

Chapter Nine

Three days after Lilly lost her freaking mind and kissed Lincoln *in her office*, she stood in the large ballroom of Enchanted Dance. The locally owned dance studio catered to everyone, from toddlers all the way up to adults. The sisters who owned and ran the studio for the past three decades provided classes in many styles of dance, from tap to ballet, hip-hop to belly dancing, and, of course, ballroom.

Mile High Happiness had worked out a contract with the studio to provide a free class to all their couples. It benefited both companies. They were able to offer their brides and grooms a free dance lesson, something most people jumped at when they were preparing for a formal event where the first dance tended to be a big thing, and the studio saw a boost in enrollment, as many couples signed up for a few more classes to polish their moves for the big day.

Tonight, the class was filled with various couples, Kenneth and Marie, a few members of their wedding party, and her. Normally Lilly didn't attend the free dance night, but Marie had insisted she come, and she was finding it hard to resist anything the sweet bride requested. Which was why she found herself in her favorite yellow sundress, smiling as she watched her clients try to waltz across the dance floor. Poor Kenneth had two left feet and kept stepping on Marie's toes, but the woman didn't seem to mind. If the smile on her face was any indication, Marie thought her fiancé hung the sun and moon. Who would mind a little toe smashing with a guy who could do that?

Her gaze wandered the crowd of dancers on the floor, landing on a certain man who inspired something a bit more earthy than the deep, abiding love she spied between Kenneth and Marie.

Lincoln Reid. Lust inspirer.

Heat still rose on her cheeks whenever she thought of the brazen way she'd pushed him against her office wall and taken his mouth. It hadn't been a gentle kiss. No softness or romance, but a demanding claim of her body declaring she wanted more. Even though her mind knew it was a bad idea.

Bad decisions make great stories.

Her roommate's favorite saying. But Mo didn't have to deal with Lilly's bad decision or the raging case of need it awakened in her. *Dammit!* She never should have kissed Lincoln. Again. The man was a potent keg of sexual dynamite. How could she have forgotten that one touch only made her crave more? She blamed her weakness on the constant nearness. But that was a lie. Even when she had zero contact with the man, she still wanted him, dreamed about him, desired him.

Unfortunately, the man in question harbored no such difficulties where she was concerned, if his current situation was anything to judge by. Something dark and ugly and suspiciously close to jealousy burned in her gut as Lilly watched Lincoln dance with the maid of honor, laughing at something the small, delicate woman said.

Not fair. Lilly wasn't one to judge another woman on her appearance. Besides, Lincoln was a few inches taller than her, until she put heels on. At five foot eight, she towered over most women and a number of men she'd dated. It never bothered her, but many of her dates called it quits the moment she rose from the table. She was a tall woman who liked even taller heels, so what? She didn't mind being taller than her date; unfortunately, many of them minded being shorter than her.

"Excellent form, Mr. Reid," Piper Phelps, one of the owners and tonight's instructor, praised Lincoln. "You must have taken dance before."

His lips curled. "My parents enrolled me in cotillion classes as a child."

Of course they had. The only thing Lilly's mom had ever enrolled her in was after-school care so she could have more time with her latest boyfriend. Lincoln had the perfect childhood with the perfect parents, making him the perfect man.

No!

He wasn't perfect. He liked role-playing games. She wasn't one to judge, but she could never get into that dragon-and-elf-type fantasy play. And he drank *pumpkin spice lattes*! Two people who didn't share hobbies or interests didn't last long, in her experience. That went on the noncompatible side of her list. The side that was sorely lacking but she was determined to fill.

The maid of honor laughed again at something Lincoln said, causing Lilly's gut to churn. Salacious flirt. There—she could add that to the list of why Lincoln Reid was a bad bet. Mr. No Relationships was probably trying to carry out the tired, old bang-the-maid-of-honor routine.

"She's married."

Lilly turned at the voice, startled to see Marie standing beside her. When had the woman left the dance floor? She'd been so focused on Lincoln, she'd lost sight of her bride- and groom-to-be. How unprofessional. Various forms of shame filled her, but she pasted a smile on her face as she asked, "Pardon?"

Marie tilted her head, short black hair held back with a beautiful silver headband. "Rachel." She indicated Lincoln's dance partner with a nod. "My matron of honor. She's married. To Leticia."

She had no idea where the woman was going with this, so she simply smiled brighter.

"I only mention it because you look like you want to scratch her eyes out for dancing with Lincoln."

Lilly sputtered, trying to come up with a reasonable excuse for her obvious staring. "O-Oh, no. I wasn't…" Nothing. She had absolutely nothing. "It's not like that."

Marie smiled, stepping closer to her side to speak in hushed tones as she stared at the couples on the dance floor. Specifically, Lincoln. Forcing Lilly to do the same.

"Really? Because I've seen the way you look at him."

Crap! Had she been that obvious? The last thing she needed was to get into another heap of trouble with a bride over a member of the wedding party. She'd assumed she had her thoughts and reactions to Lincoln under wraps.

"And," Marie continued, "I've seen the way he looks at you."

Now the woman had her curious. She knew how she felt about Lincoln, sort of. There were a lot of confusing feelings and emotions, but she got the gist. Or her body did, anyway. But other than his desire for another roll in the sack, she had no idea how he felt about her.

Unable to stop the question from leaving her lips, Lilly turned her head to the other woman and asked, "How?"

The bride-to-be kept her focus on her friend on the dance floor, but a small smile played on her lips as she bypassed the question. "I love Lincoln. He's my best friend after Kenneth. Like a brother to me. He's been at our side through thick and thin. He was a rock for both me and Kenneth when I got sick and was going through chemo, always there to make me smile or hold me when I cried. He even held Kenneth a time or two. He's our family."

She understood that. Maybe not to the depths that those three experienced, but she, Mo, and Pru had been through a lot together. Death and heartbreak had touched their lives, and she and her friends had always been there for one another. She understood the bond Marie felt to Lincoln.

"He had a rough patch himself a few years ago."

Lincoln? Always smiling and joking, carefree Lincoln had a rough patch? She couldn't see it. The man breezed through life like he didn't have a care in the world. Like he wore some kind of bad-news Teflon coating. She couldn't imagine the cheerful guy experiencing a dark period.

C'mon, Lil. Life isn't all sunshine and rainbows. You know that, even if Mo doesn't.

Yes, she had firsthand knowledge of the misery life could throw a person's way. Naive of her to think Lincoln lived a life of carefree bliss. The man had a close friend who beat cancer. Of course he'd had some dark moments. But somehow she knew Marie wasn't speaking of Lincoln's reaction to her own illness.

"What happened?" The question was out of her mouth before she could really think about it. She didn't need to know more about this man. Knowing more would make him more human, more…appealing. But she couldn't seem to stop her curiosity from getting the better of her.

"Not my story to tell." Marie's gaze was still fixated on Lincoln, though her smile slipped a little. "But it scared him off relationships and love. He hasn't dated much since. Or smiled." The woman's head turned to her, eyes considering.

"But when he looks at you, I see it again."

She held her breath. "What?"

The smile returned to the bride's face, bright this time, hopeful. "Happiness."

Well, damn.

"I like you, Lilly. You're sweet and kind, and I know we're paying you, so it might all be an act, but I don't think it is." Marie tilted her head, staring with those dark, knowing eyes. "You care."

Her head bobbed up and down of its own accord. It was true. She did care. Not just about making a paycheck but about her clients. Even the ones she knew were doomed to fail. Those she sometimes cared about more because she could see the disaster coming but felt powerless to do anything about it. All she could do was give them the day of their dreams and hope things worked out in the end.

"He's a great guy," Marie continued. "And he deserves a great woman."

Did the bride-to-be mean her? And if she did, what did that mean for Lilly's no-dating-members-of-the-wedding-party rule? The last disaster happened because she'd kept her relationship a secret. At the request of the guy. Stupid. That should have been her first red flag, but she'd been blinded by her emotions and hadn't been using her head. Mistake number two.

But this situation was different. The bride herself seemed to be pushing the two of them together. She was fairly certain Marie was still unaware of Lilly and Lincoln's one-night stand. If the woman did know, would she be more or less eager to help make this match? And what was that thing Marie said about heartbreak? Could it have something to do with Lincoln's distaste of long-term relationships?

It's not like they shared much of their lives the night they were together, but the thought of Lincoln having a secret made her gut clench. The last secret a guy kept from her almost destroyed her and those she loved.

Her head was spinning, and she hadn't even participated in any of the twirls or spins currently being demonstrated on the dance floor.

In the end, none of it mattered. Whatever tragic event happened in Lincoln's past had pushed him away from meaningful relationships. He had mentioned a time or two not being big on long-term commitment. Their night together might have been a first for both of them, but it seemed Lincoln was more Netflix and Chill, whereas Lilly was Hulu and Commitment.

Their relationship goals didn't match. Probably the biggest marker on her list proving their paper match was a no go, which should make her happy. Then what was this sharp twinge of sadness filling her chest?

"Hey, sweetheart, sorry about that." Kenneth arrived at Marie's side, kissing her cheek as he slipped his cell phone into his pocket. "My mom had a few questions about the rehearsal dinner."

So that's why the two had left the dance floor. At the reminder of why she was really here—to work, not to ogle a man she shouldn't want—Lilly turned her smile to Kenneth. "Anything I can help with?"

Other than recommendations for venues and sometimes bookings, the rehearsal dinners were largely left up to the couple, as most in-laws handled that aspect of the wedding. Since the wedding was being held outside of the city in the mountains, Kenneth's parents had contacted Lilly a month ago to garner suggestions, and she'd provided the couple a few of the best caterers in the area.

"Nope." Kenneth smiled at her. "Mom just wanted to make sure she had the head count right." He nuzzled his fiancée's ear. "You ready to get back out there?"

Marie giggled, her shoulder raising as Kenneth gave her tiny love nips along her neck. The moment was so intimate that Lilly turned her eyes back to the dance floor to give the couple a bit of privacy. Nothing she wasn't used to. Soon-to-be married couples were often so in love, so wrapped up in their own happiness, they tended to forget other people were in the room with them. A tiny love bite was nothing compared to the few instances where a couple's PDA had gotten so out of control she actually had to audibly remind the couple she stood a few feet away.

"Actually," Marie answered, "I need to talk to Rachel about the bachelorette party. Can you go grab her for me?"

Like the lovesick puppy he was, Kenneth placed a kiss to his fiancée's cheek and hurried off to do her bidding. Lilly watched as he weaved among dancing couples to reach Lincoln and Rachel's side, tapping his friend on the shoulder and sharing a few words. When the man pointed their way, Rachel smiled, nodding and giving Lincoln a hug. A very friendly and long hug, in Lilly's opinion.

Married, Lilly. To a woman. Get your ugly jealous head out of your ass.

Ugh! She needed help.

Kenneth hurried back over with Rachel, the woman spotted Lilly and smiled.

"Hi, Lilly. How's it going?"

She'd met Rachel at the bridesmaid dress fitting a few weeks ago. They hadn't conversed much, but she was very nice and seemed genuine. Which made Lilly feel all the more awful for her petty and completely unwarranted jealousy.

"Hello, Rachel. I'm doing fine. You looked beautiful out there."

Lilly had two left feet, and neither of them could dance a step.

"Thanks. I met my wife line dancing. We still go every

Friday night."

"Excuse me." Marie grabbed her friend's hand. "I need to steal my matron of honor for a moment." A sly smile overtook the bride-to-be's face. "Oh dear, it looks like Lincoln is all alone out there. Lilly, why don't you go dance with him?"

"Oh, no. I couldn't." Not if she wanted to keep her distance—and her clothes on.

"Don't be silly," Marie insisted. "He needs a partner. You can't leave him out there by himself."

Her logic was sound, but Lilly smelled a setup. Especially after the conversation they'd just had. No way was Marie pushing her toward Lincoln just so the guy wouldn't be alone on the dance floor.

"Kenneth, will you take her over there, please?"

"Babe," Kenneth whispered into Marie's ear, just loud enough for Lilly to catch his hesitation. "Are you sure that's a good idea? I mean, after—"

"It's fine, honey." Marie batted her eyes at her fiancé, who looked slightly apprehensive but agreed to her request.

"Come on." Kenneth gently took her arm and started to lead her across the room, weaving her among the twirling couples.

"Oh, but I—"

Her protests were cut off as they arrived in front of the man in question.

"Hey, Lincoln." Kenneth glanced back to Marie with a puzzled frown but, at her wave, turned back and smiled at his friend. "I found you a new dance partner."

"Did you now?"

Pale hazel eyes lit up, a smile curving Lincoln's lips as he stared directly into her eyes. With their minimal height difference and her three-inch heels, they were on even footing. She might even be a half inch taller than him. Didn't seem to bother the man one bit. He stood there, grinning at her like a fool. No. Not a fool. Like a predator about to devour his prey. And at the moment, she felt very much like prey. An offering by a sweet but meddling woman in love. Why did people in love always try and set up everyone they knew? Just because they were happy and lucky in love didn't mean everyone else would be, too.

A buzzing sound came from Kenneth, and he dropped her arm to dig his phone out of his pocket.

"It's my mom again. I better take this." He brought the phone to his ear, leaving the dance floor with a wave. "Hey, Mom. What? No. Cousin Barry is allergic to shellfish, not peanuts."

Lilly stared after Kenneth as he left, her attention catching on Marie talking to Rachel. The woman noticed her stare and smiled, giving her a wink and thumbs-up. Very different energy than the weird vibe coming off Kenneth as he led her over here. It seemed not everyone was on the Lilly-and-Lincoln train. In all the months she'd known the couple, this was the first thing she'd seen them not 100 percent agree on. The realization left a sick sense of dread in the pit of her stomach.

She turned back to Lincoln to find him smiling at her, a question filling his soft gaze. One she had precisely zero answer to. She was trying to be strong in resisting him, but she had about fifty-fifty support and opposition from the people around her right now, and the even split was not helping her give a firm no or yes either way.

Because if she gave this man her body again, she feared she just might lose her heart.

Chapter Ten

Lincoln smiled as Lilly gave him a considering stare. "What?"

She shook her head. "Your friends are about as subtle as mine."

He laughed, a deep, loud rumble that filled his chest and warmed his belly. She had that right. The past two weeks, Marie had been making some not-so-subtle hints about Lilly and what a great catch she was. Preaching to the choir. What his friend didn't know was he had firsthand knowledge of exactly how dynamite the woman could be. And not only in bed. Every moment he'd spent in her presence had been a fascinating discovery of a fierce and feisty woman who appeared cool and controlled on the outside but had a wild and passionate spirit burning within.

She could stand to loosen up on her rigid rules, and she definitely needed to join the age of updated technology, but he supposed no one was perfect.

"Shall we?" He held out his hand.

Lilly glanced to the dance floor, a slight grimace turning those sweet red lips. "Trust me, you do not want to dance with me."

Actually, he'd like nothing more at the moment. While he'd much rather take her back to bed and pleasure her until neither of them could walk straight the next day, they were in public without a bed in sight, and that desire would have to wait.

"I don't?" He tilted his head at her assuredness.

She gave a soft laugh. "I am a terrible dancer. I have zero rhythm, and more than one person has accused me of breaking their baby toe."

He highly doubted the woman could dance poorly enough to break a toe. Unless she danced in steel boots. A quick glance to her feet revealed a pair of sleek and shiny blue high heels with tiny skyscraper picks that somehow held her up, making her his exact height. Maybe even half an inch taller. Lincoln didn't care. At five foot ten, he wasn't the tallest guy in any room, and he'd dated women in the past who matched or even exceeded his height. Never bothered him. Just made the journey to heaven a shorter one.

"In those killer shoes?" He whistled. "Stab me, maybe, but I doubt you could break anything."

She glanced down with a smile. "You like my shoes?"

If he liked them any more, there'd be an uncomfortable tenting situation going on. As it was, he was having a hard time controlling his body's reaction to this woman. The shoes were only one part of her alluring look tonight. The pale yellow dress, which complemented the shoes in color so perfectly he was sure she bought them together, clung to her curves, hugging every delectable inch of her body from the scoop of the collar, which was modest and yet revealed just the hint of teasing cleavage, to where it nipped in at her waist—a waist he vividly remembered grasping in his hands as she rode him with wild abandon. It fanned out, hitting her just above her knees, revealing the mile-long legs he still dreamed about. Having those beauties wrapped around him as he thrust into her was a memory branded on his soul.

"I love them." He lifted his hand. "And I would love to dance with you in them. I promise not to mention any injuries you might inflict, even if there's blood drawn."

She laughed. "Okay, but don't say I didn't warn you."

Ten minutes later, he struggled to hold in the affirmation of her warning.

"I told you." Lilly chuckled as he grimaced when she stepped on his toe for the fifth time. "I am a terrible dancer."

The instructor had come by three times to help, but it seemed even the dancer with decades of experience and teaching under her dance belt had pegged Lilly as a lost cause. Not him, though.

"Put your feet on mine."

One dark, perfectly sculpted eyebrow rose. Her glasses slipped down her nose a bit.

"Seriously? I've been stepping on them for the past ten minutes, and now you want me to full-on crush your feet?"

Releasing the arm he had on her waist, he brought his hand up to gently push the dark frames back up her nose with a single finger. Bright green eyes blinked behind the clear glass at his action. "No. I don't want you to crush them, but I do want you to gently place your feet on mine."

She did as he requested, grumbling as she did so. "I feel like a kid with her father at a daddy-daughter dance."

He returned the hand to her waist, resuming the slight sway, moving to the steps of the dance much easier now that her feet were purposely on top of his.

"Dance a lot this way with your dad as a kid?"

Her eyes focused on the wall behind his head. "No. I never knew my father. He ran out on my mom when she got pregnant with me."

Damn, that sucked. He could never imagine abandoning

a kid. He'd always wanted a family of his own. Past tense. Now he was glad he and Jessa never got to that point in their marriage. After what happened, he was grateful they didn't bring a kid into that mess.

"I'm sorry."

She shrugged as if it didn't matter, but it did. He could tell in the way her body tightened at the subject.

"How are you enjoying Colorado?"

Not the subtlest of subject changes, but he understood. Difficult pasts were hard to talk about. Wasn't like he wanted to open up and spew all the crap that had happened to him a few years ago. He was surprised she even shared as much with him as she did.

"I love it," he answered. "The mountains are amazing. I moved from Nebraska, and the closest thing we had to a mountain was Panorama Point, which is a little over five thousand feet in elevation."

She laughed, the sound brightening the room. "That's not a mountain. That's a speed bump. We have fifty-three fourteeners in Colorado."

"What's a fourteener?" he asked, carefully spinning them away from an elderly couple that was dancing a bit too close. A difficult move with someone on his toes, but he managed.

"Fourteen thousand feet in elevation."

He whistled. "Now that's a mountain."

"Makes for great skiing."

He shrugged. "Don't really like the cold. I prefer the summer months, hiking, camping. Warm-weather activities."

Her arm tightened around his neck, fingers absently playing with the short hairs at his nape. It was driving him insane, and he was fairly certain she wasn't even aware she was doing it.

"I hate camping, and I'm not much for hiking, but give me a snowy, slick hill to fly down at unwise speeds, and I'm there." Her voice took on a resigned tone, eyes focusing on something internal as she stared at his chest. "I suppose this is a good thing. Another mismatch to add to the list."

"What list?" Mismatch? What was she talking about?

Her gaze snapped back up to his, eyes clear as a stilted smile curled her lips. "Huh? Oh, nothing. It's silly."

He let the thing about her dad go, but this, this had nothing to do with past pains, and he had a sneaking suspicion it had everything to do with him. So he pressed.

"I could use some silly right now."

She tilted her head, considering him for a moment before shrugging and answering, "I'm compiling a list of our differences to show how unsuited we are to each other."

Wait, what? She was making a list to prove they wouldn't work? First time he'd ever heard that. He had to admit, it stung a bit. Okay, a lot.

He slowed their movement until they were simply swaying in place at the back edge of the dance floor. The instructor was occupied with the other couples, having given up on them a while ago. Marie was still talking to Rachel, and Kenneth hadn't returned from his phone call to his mother. Everyone was focused on themselves, but all his focus zeroed in on the fascinating, confounding woman in his arms.

"You're coming up with reasons we shouldn't be together."

"I'm not coming up with them," she huffed. "I'm simply acknowledging them and keeping track."

"Because…"

She stared at him like he was the slowest man on the planet. "Because people who don't work out on paper rarely work out in the long term."

What the hell kind of backward thinking was that?

"And you know this from your years of wedding planning?"

Her jaw tightened. "I know this from life."

All right. There was a backstory there, but he wasn't going to hold his breath for it. Getting this woman to open up was like solving the P versus NP problem.

"Then chemistry means nothing?" He didn't want to push too hard, because he knew she'd walk away, but he did want to know what made this woman tick. Why she hid behind this wall of control.

"Chemistry is simply a case of lust that makes people lose sight of the big picture. It's a momentary distraction that blinds people to the long term."

Pretty cynical view, but he didn't think she'd appreciate him pointing that out.

"Let me get this straight—you're saying because I like camping and you like skiing, we shouldn't explore this thing we got going?" Never before had he been so on edge waiting for the answer to a question.

Lilly shook her head, dark hair cascading around her shoulders with the movement. He remembered that hair, how soft it felt slipping through his fingers. The way it tickled his jaw, tiny filaments sticking in his scruff as her mouth devoured his. Momentary distraction, his ass. It was weeks later, and he was still thinking about it.

"That, among other issues. We might work for a night or two in bed."

Yeah. They'd already proven that fact.

"But beyond that, I'm afraid we're incompatible."

He'd get to the *other issues* later—for now, he wanted to remind her of the ways in which they were very much compatible. Tugging her closer, he brushed his lips up the side of her jaw, grazing a barely-there kiss just under her ear as he whispered, "Not completely incompatible."

He felt her shiver in his arms, her nipples tightening against the thin material of her dress, pressing into his chest through the silky shirt he wore. Her breath came out in rapid, tiny pants. A sound he remembered fondly from their night together. Ecstatic at the fact that she was just as affected as he was—no matter her valiant attempts to deny what was between them—he grinned.

"After all, we both like pinball."

A laugh escaped her lips, and she nudged him with her shoulder. "Jerk." But the word held no anger.

He pulled back to stare into her face again. She was smiling now, but there was a twinge of sadness to the expression.

"You kick ass at pinball, fixed my computer in ten minutes, dance like a dream, and make me laugh." She sighed. "Can you please just have one flaw I can pinpoint to keep myself in check?"

He shrugged, in no way wanting to help her with this particular dilemma. "I snore?"

"No, you don't."

He grinned at catching her acknowledging their night together.

"I like eating cookies in bed."

She wrinkled her nose. "Gross. Food belongs in the kitchen, not the bedroom. You'd get crumbs everywhere."

"Not if you have a dog in bed to clean them up."

"Double gross. Pets do not belong in bed. And anyway, I prefer cats."

Dang, that little factoid was probably going on her ridiculous list, too.

"Okay, class, that ends our time together tonight," the instructor called.

The music shut off, and all the couples on the dance floor stopped moving. Though he hated to do it, Lincoln stopped as well. The moment Lilly stepped out of his arms, they felt empty without her warmth, and he had no idea what to do with that.

"Well, um, thank you for letting me crush your feet."

He wiggled his toes in his shoes. "Not a broken bone among them." She smiled, and even though he knew the answer, he couldn't stop himself from asking, "Need a ride home?"

Her teeth came out to worry her bottom lip. A move that hardened his body. Everywhere.

He wanted nothing more than to reach over and free that poor lip, soothe her tiny teeth marks with his tongue, and kiss her until she forgot all about wedding clients and lists and matching on paper. Until the only thing she remembered was how explosive they were together. How right it felt.

"I think…" She took a deep breath, exhaling with a shake of her head. "I think that would be a very bad idea."

He shrugged. "Bad ideas can have great results."

Her lips curled up in a wry smile. "I'm parked in the lot downstairs. They tow if you leave a car overnight. Better not risk it."

"Ouch." He placed a hand to his chest in mock pain. "I'm not good enough to risk a tow fee. Seems I need to work on my bedroom skills."

She rolled her eyes, the smile growing wider. "Good night, Lincoln. Thank you for the dance."

"Night, Lilly. The pleasure was mine." And hers, he hoped.

She started to walk away.

"Lilly." She turned at his call. "Just so you know. I totally would have made your night worth the towing fee."

Her brow furrowed. She glanced around the room, but most everyone had left already. The teacher was at the sound system, fiddling with the playlist on her phone, and Kenneth had come back and was busy conversing with Rachel and Marie at the entrance to the large ballroom. He watched her take everything into account until a determined look settled on her face. Her gaze swung back to him, and she took a few forceful steps to stand in front of him. She stood toe to toe—thankfully not on them this time—and stared him directly in the eyes.

"You, Lincoln Reid, are a very bad idea...and totally worth any towing fee."

Then she tilted her chin up and placed her soft lips over his. He didn't even have time to react to the kiss before she pulled back. She pointed a finger in his face.

"This has to stop happening."

He did not agree in any way with that statement. He hoped it kept happening. That and more.

"Ugh!"

She threw her hands in the air at his reply of a grin, turning and storming off, muttering something about a stupid, sexy man being impossible to resist. That was twice now she'd kissed him. Twice she fell victim to the chemistry she claimed to denounce. Dare he hope the third time would be the charm that led her back to his bed?

"Dude, did I just see what I thought I saw?"

He turned as Kenneth walked up to his side.

"Depends on what you thought you saw."

"Looked like Lilly just planted one on you."

He stared at the woman in question as she stopped by Marie's side, asking her something. Marie smiled, shaking her head and grabbing Lilly in a fierce hug. He saw Lilly stiffen, awkwardly patting his friend on the back. The woman did not handle physical expression well.

Except with me.

True. She had no issue being relaxed in his arms.

"So, did I?" Kenneth prodded. "See you kiss my wedding planner?"

He shook his head. "I didn't kiss her." Technically the

truth.

"But she kissed you?"

He stared at his best friend. The guy who was less like a pal and more like a brother. The man he usually told everything to. But not this. Lilly might not be able to deny the chemistry between them—she might be fighting a losing battle, and he might enjoy watching her struggle—but he'd be damned if he did anything to upset her. Revealing anything about their night together or any incident that happened since would hurt her. He knew this instinctively. She valued her professionalism, her business, and he would never do anything to put that in jeopardy. So he simply stared at his friend silently.

"Okay." Kenneth nodded, taking the hint. "I saw nothing, but just know I think Lilly is great and all, but..."

"But what?"

His friend rubbed the back of his neck. Kenneth hated confrontation, but the guy never shied away from talking about something that was important.

"You two don't really have a lot in common, and..." Kenneth's gaze softened. "I just don't want to see you get hurt again."

Jessa's betrayal hadn't only impacted Lincoln; his friends had taken it hard, too. At one time, they'd all been the fantastic foursome, the perfect couple friends. His ex's cheating ruined their core group dynamic, and he knew his buddy still harbored anger on Lincoln's behalf.

"Don't worry, man." He slapped Kenneth on the back. "It's nothing that serious."

Kenneth narrowed his eyes. "I don't know if that makes it better or worse."

He shrugged. "It makes it what it is."

And what it was at the moment was a whole lotta nothing. Because he was part of a wedding Lilly was planning. But after the wedding…could he convince her that this explosive chemistry they had deserved another night or two of exploration? He wasn't asking for forever. He didn't let his heart get involved like that anymore. Even if the thing did tug uncomfortably in his chest every time the intriguing woman was near.

Sex only, because he couldn't give anything more. He just couldn't.

Chapter Eleven

Lincoln stepped into his apartment, sweat dripping down his forehead into his eyes. He swiped at the moisture with his forearm, tossing his keys into the small bowl on the kitchen table. One thing he'd learned in his few short weeks living in Denver: the city had some awesome running trails. Between the Cherry Creek Trail and the abundant parks, it was a runner's dream city.

He shrugged off his soft-shell running jacket, stripping the long-sleeved thermal shirt underneath off as well. When the weather got really bad, he'd run on the small treadmill he bought a few years ago, but he hated running in place. He found it boring as hell. So barring below-zero temperatures or a few feet of snow, Lincoln headed outside every morning for a mind-clearing run.

And boy had he needed to clear his mind lately. After Lilly planted those sweet lips on him the other night—again— his brain hadn't been able to stop thinking of the smart, sexy woman. Remembering their night together, imagining all the things he wanted to do again and all the things he wanted to do for the first time. If only she'd agree to another go-around.

He understood her need to keep their relationship professional. Okay, he didn't. He wasn't her client; his friends were. But he respected it. If she had a personal rule about comingling with members of her wedding parties, he could abide by that. And it was a personal rule, if her business partner Mo was anything to go by. Her other partner, Pru, might still be on the fence, judging by the hesitant looks he caught her giving him, but Mo had practically thrown them together the other day when he came over to fix their computer. She didn't seem to have a problem with her dating someone involved in a wedding they were hired to plan, so why did Lilly?

Something he should ask but had held back from. The answer was sure to be a deep and personal one, most likely filled with pain and bad memories. He was still working through his own issues regarding a bad relationship experience; he wasn't sure he was ready or able to help anyone else with theirs. Knowing why Lilly had a rule against dating client-adjacent people would take them from the playful, yet powerful, lust-driven connection they shared to something deeper. More real. Lincoln didn't know if he was ready for that yet. Or ever again.

He hopped into the shower, sudsing and scrubbing the frozen sweat from his body. The hot water pounding on his back and shoulders loosened the tense muscles. Steam soon filled the tiny bathroom, creating a sauna-like atmosphere. Who needed the gym when he could enjoy a hot steam in the privacy of his own home?

He shut off the water, stepping out of the shower and toweling dry. Wiping the condensation from the mirror, he glanced at himself, raising a hand to rub at the dark scruff that had turned from the beginnings of a beard to a full-fledged face warmer. He hated shaving. No matter what he tried—creams, oils, the electric or manual razors—he always got razor burn. Damn sensitive skin. Luckily, his vocation didn't care if he was clean-shaven or not. Score one for being a computer geek.

Maybe he'd let his beard grow out a little. He was in the land of hipsters and homebrews, after all. If he got himself a flannel shirt, he could fit right in with the other lumbersexuals he'd seen around town. But he drew the line at a man bun. He didn't have the dedication long hair required.

Making his way out of the bathroom to his bedroom, he checked the time. He had a few hours before Kenneth's bachelor party started. Marie and her bridesmaids were having their party at the same time. Everyone was meeting at the end of the night at some bar so the couple could go home together. He made a mental note to turn his music up extra loud tonight. Unfortunately, he'd discovered sound did indeed carry through the floors.

At least he knew his friends were happy.

Very happy.

• • •

Hey, what are you up to tonight?

Lilly glanced at her phone, reading the message lighting up the screen. She paused the show she'd been watching, brow furrowing as she glanced at the name of the sender.

Aren't you supposed to be at Kenneth's bachelor party right now?

I am, Lincoln's text came back. *Wanna see a picture of the strippers?*

She'd chosen that unfortunate moment to take a sip of her soda. Liquid came out her nose as she choked on the sip. The bubbles popped, irritating her nostrils. Thank God Mo was out tonight. She didn't want to have to explain why she just inhaled carbonated sugar water.

No! she texted back, swiping at her damp face with the back of her sleeve. *I most certainly do not.*

How the hell could he think she'd want to see some scantily clad women dancing for skeevy drunk pervs? She knew quite a few erotic dancers, and they were extremely talented. Mo had badgered her into taking a free intro pole-dancing class, and she fell flat on her face. Tweaked the heck out of her shoulder. Never went back. Those women had talent and deserved much more recognition than they received.

You sure?

Three tiny dots popped up, indicating he was about to send her something. She hoped it wasn't a picture. Or maybe it'd be good if it was. If Lincoln turned out to be some misogynistic creep who thought women's bodies only existed for his visual pleasure and that snapping pics in a strip club was okay, she could nip this weird lustful crush thing in the bud for sure.

A picture arrived on her phone, making her want to laugh and cry at the same time. The screen showed not a woman in pasties and a thong but a small silver can with the words *Wood Stripper* prominent on the label.

Dammit. How could she be happy and upset at the same time? He wasn't a creep. Far from it. The man actually had a wicked sense of humor. Oh, she was in so much trouble.

Oh ha ha mister funny man.

I think so. ;)

He ended the text with a smiling winking face.

She knew she shouldn't engage. The more time she spent with the man, the more she wanted to have him again. But they weren't even in the same room. Texting wasn't spending time together, right? It wasn't even a phone call, just simple words on a screen. He could be anyone. She could resist that, right? What could be the harm in a little back-and-forth texting?

Wood stripping? What a wild party you guys are having.

She was in it now.

She held the phone tightly in her grip, staring at the three tiny dots until they turned into a message her eyes greedily devoured.

We started with lunch and a brewery tour of Wynkoop, then we headed to this shop that lets you make your own woodworking projects.

That sounded fun. If you were into beer and woodworking. She wasn't, but it sounded a hell of a lot better than getting trashed and ogling half-naked women to celebrate finding the love of your life. Honestly, she never understood the whole stripper-for-your-bachelor/bachelorette-party thing. Wouldn't it make more sense to have that for a breakup party?

The ladies hit up a spa and are doing a wine and painting party. Then we're all meeting up later at some bar.

Now that sounded like something Lilly would totally be into. A nice massage and steam followed by delicious wine and creativity? Sign her up. She knew she liked Marie and Kenneth for a reason. The couple had good taste in recreational activities.

Sounds like fun. What are you making?

She took another sip of her soda, carefully, as she waited for his reply.

A birdhouse. At least it's supposed to be.

Moments later, another text came through, and she once again choked on her drink. Thankfully, it was most of the way down her throat, so it didn't shoot up her nose this time. The sad looking structure in no way resembled a birdhouse. The roof was askew, one side higher than the other. The walls were uneven, adding to the lopsided-roof issue. Tiny nails stuck out of the wood at dangerous angles, and glue oozed out of seams, dripping down the unevenly stained tiny wooden house. Any poor bird that tried to land on that thing would cut their wings to shreds.

Thank you, she texted.

For what?

For revealing one of your faults to me. She laughed as she typed. *You may be a wiz at computers, a dynamite dancer, and amazing in bed, but you can't woodwork to save a life.*

There was a slight pause before his reply came.

You think I'm amazing in bed?

Crap! Had she really typed that? She scrolled up a bit—dammit, yes she had. Well, it wasn't like the man didn't already know. She was pretty sure she left scratch marks on his back after their night together. Bite marks, too.

Stop fishing for compliments and get back to your party.

He sent her a winking kissy face emoji with a heart. Lilly rolled her eyes, even if a part of her giggled in girlish glee. A ridiculous part. She needed to get a handle on this crush thing before it got out of control. Starting anything serious with Lincoln was a bad idea.

Why? She chided her inner voice for being a dope.

Lincoln made her feel far too much. He wasn't just sexy and great in bed. He was also sweet and funny, kind and generous. He was someone she could see herself getting emotionally invested in, and that was bad. She knew all too well what happened when you emotionally invested in someone. They stomped on your heart and crushed your dreams. How many times had she held her mother as the woman sobbed over her latest disaster? How many times had the woman assured her daughter this next guy was different, the one, only to have her heart stomped on all over again?

No. Lilly knew the only successful relationship was one built on mutual understanding, compromise, and commonality. Sure, she wanted to like her future husband, but all that passionate-emotional-love stuff wouldn't do. Not for her.

I don't have to love him to have sex with him again.

An interesting thought. One she shouldn't be entertaining but was. Blame it on the lateness of the evening, the loneliness she'd been feeling recently, or the memory of how exquisite he made her feel in bed. She could blame it on the full moon—that wouldn't occur for another week—but in the end, it was only a thought. One she knew she couldn't act on while he was a member of one of her wedding parties.

So why was she picking up her phone as she lay in bed? Bringing up their text exchange as the darkness of the night surrounded her? Sending him a text well after midnight when any normal person would be sleeping soundly?

You get home safe?

There. She was simply checking on him. Making sure he and the others got home safe. She waited, the glow of the tiny screen illuminating nothing but her hand in the dark room.

Home safe and sound with my stereo at full blast.

What an odd tidbit to include. Had they brought the party home to Lincoln's place? She really shouldn't ask. He'd made it home safe. That's all she texted to say. But…

Still partying?

No. I live below Kenneth and Marie, and let's just say the happy couple is very happy and very loud.

She laughed. Poor Lincoln. She, Mo, and Pru made a pact that all nookie would be held at the other party's house or when roommates were not around.

Poor you. Can I do anything to distract you?

You can tell me what you're wearing.

She hesitated, working through a checklist in her mind. She couldn't get involved with Lincoln, not while he was technically part of her clientele. But then again, she had gotten involved with him. On the other hand, she hadn't known he was the best man of her current wedding, so no one could fault her, and Marie seemed more than okay with her and Lincoln being together...ugh! Her head was hurting trying to sort all this out.

Bottom line, she couldn't be physically involved with him while facilitating this wedding. But technically, there was no physicality in what they were currently doing. A few words on a screen wasn't physical. Heck, it wasn't even vocal. It was simply...words.

I'm kidding, Lilly.

She bit her lip, mind made up as she hurried to text him back before he turned off his phone and went to bed.

A nightshirt and panties.

There was a pause before those three tiny dots appeared, followed by the words, *What color panties?*

She laughed. Such a guy. She quickly typed back.

Black boy shorts. What are you wearing?

Don't you remember? I sleep in the buff.

She did remember that, but she hadn't realized it was an everyday occurrence for him. Another text from Lincoln appeared.

I wish I was there with you.

She licked her lips, boldness rising with each word she typed out.

What would you do?

First I'd kiss you until you couldn't breathe.

She was having a hard time with that already.

Then I'd slowly strip your nightshirt off and work my way down to your amazing breasts. Giving each one the worship it deserves with my mouth.

Her nipples tightened, memories of Lincoln doing just that during their night together filling her mind. She remembered how soft his mouth was, the sharp sting of the tiny love bites he gave, the heavy ache that settled between her legs. It was there now, just from a few words and a memory.

Another line of text appeared.

I'd slowly work my way down your body, peeling those sexy panties off you so I could place my mouth on the heaven between your legs and taste your sweetness again.

A moan left her lips as she slipped her hand into her panties, stroking herself, wishing it was Lincoln there instead of her own hand.

Are you touching yourself, sweetheart?

One hand tending to her business, she texted with a single thumb. A bit awkward, but she managed.

Yes.

Good. The dots reappeared for a moment before more words came through. *Imagine it's me, touching you, pleasing you, filling you.*

She didn't have to imagine. She remembered. In vivid detail. He might think she'd forgotten or shrugged off that night, but it was always there in the back of her mind, screaming at her for more. More Lincoln.

Touch yourself, Lincoln, she typed out. *Pretend it's me wrapped around your cock.*

With pleasure.

She continued to stroke herself, imagining it was Lincoln quickening her breath, raising her heartbeat. Another line of text appeared.

Damn, sweetheart, you set me off even when I can't see or hear you. Just the thought of you, the memory has me close to exploding.

Fair enough. She was so close to the edge right now, all she had to do was imagine his sexy smile and she'd be done. Quickening her strokes, she texted back.

Do it. Come with me, Lincoln.

Yes, Lilly.

With those simple two words, an affirmation and her

name, Lilly cried out, her body tightening with her release, pleasure exploding from deep within as she lay in bed alone but not truly alone. The words of the man she couldn't get out of her mind flying from his small screen to hers. A part of him with her, though they were halfway across the city.

I have a confession, she texted. *I've never sexted before.*

She waited, a small amount of embarrassment now filling her at the brazenness of the act. His reply sent a whoosh of relief through her.

Neither have I, but I gotta say, it was hot as hell. You're hot as hell.

She laughed, deciding not to worry about what had just happened. It was just phone sex. Not even that, really. Text sex. That didn't break her rule. Everything was fine.

Thank you. Right back at you.

He sent her a winking emoji followed by the heart-eyes face. With a shake of her head, she decided to send the exact same combo back.

Good night, Lincoln.

Good night, Lilly.

Placing her phone on the nightstand, she settled against her pillow, sleep coming easy now that her body was sated. Tomorrow she might see deeper consequences to what occurred tonight, but for now she was going to slip off to sleep and enjoy the sweet dreams of a man who made her laugh, smile, and lose herself with nothing but a few typed words.

Chapter Twelve

The sharp ring of her cell phone woke Lilly from one of the best night's sleeps she'd had in weeks. In fact, the last time she'd slept this soundly was the first night she and Lincoln had sex.

We didn't have sex. We sexted. Big difference.

In person or through typed message, it didn't seem to matter. Apparently, just imagining making love to the man had her feeling more rested than a full eight hours ever did.

No. Not making love. Having sex. Big difference, Lilly Walsh.

And she'd do well to remember it. Childish notions of true love and soulmates were best left to people who believe in that crap. Like Mo.

Reaching out to her nightstand, she slapped her hand around until it encountered her phone. Normally, she was a morning person, but she had stayed up a bit later than usual last night. The reason for her rare night-owl behavior made her lips curl up into a satisfied grin. Maybe it was Lincoln calling to start the morning off with a little upgrade to phone sex. She could handle that. Still not in person; technically, still not breaking her rule.

The logic had fault in it somewhere, but she'd reason it out after she woke up more.

She glanced at the screen, and all her hopes of morning nookie vanished. Her libido took a crashing dive into nonexistence as she accepted the call and put the phone to her ear.

"Hi, Mom."

Speaking of people who believed in all that soul mate nonsense.

"Lilly, baby, you didn't call me back."

She winced, remembering the message Mo had given her last week. "Right, sorry, Mom. I've been…busy."

Not true. She'd simply forgotten her mother was getting married. Again. Or blocked it out. Possibly a bit of both.

"Not too busy to help your mother plan her wedding to her one true love, I hope."

Considering the woman had had several "one true loves" over the course of her lifetime, Lilly wondered how her mother managed to find time for anything else. She certainly hadn't found time for her daughter.

Not entirely fair. Her mother hadn't been neglectful or abusive, she'd just been…very occupied with her own life. Lilly always had food to eat and clothes to wear, but there was never any help with homework. No parent at her school events to cheer her on. No one to talk to about friend drama, struggles with insecurities, boy troubles.

Though spending her childhood watching her mother go through men like tissues, she'd never been all that big on dating anyway.

"Aren't you living in Napa right now?" Her mother's location always changed with her latest man.

"Yes, but Stavros wants a Rocky Mountain destination

wedding." Her mother's light laughter rang in her ear. "The man likes to pretend he's a Wild West cowboy. We were thinking something in the fall, when the leaves turn those brilliant gold and ruby colors. When I told him my daughter puts together little weddings in Colorado, he insisted we hire you."

She didn't "put together little weddings." She ran a very successful wedding planning business with two other competent and professional women. To hear her mom tell it, they were little girls running around playing dress up in their mothers' wedding gowns. You'd think a woman who'd had multiple weddings over the years would understand how much work went into planning one.

"He's such a sweet man," her mother continued. "He treats me like a princess."

So did all the others, right before things went to hell and they up and left.

"That's great, Mom."

It wasn't that she didn't want her mother to be happy; she just wished the woman wouldn't base all her happiness on the love of someone else. Love, passion, romance—they all fizzled out in the end. For most people. There were the lucky few who somehow stumbled upon that other human who completed them in every way.

"How about it, baby? Do you think you can help create your mother's perfect day?"

She'd done it twice before. No reason she couldn't do it again. All she had to do was smile and nod and listen to her mother profess her undying love yet again. So what if every one of her mother's marriages pushed her further down into disillusionment? At least her mom was happy. That young girl, the one who spent hours wiping the tears from her mother's face after yet another man left her heartbroken, still lived inside Lilly. And that part of her would do whatever it took to see her mother smile, even if she knew it likely wouldn't last.

Talk about mommy issues.

"Let me talk to Pru and Mo, but I'm sure we can work something out."

"Wonderful! Stavros will be so pleased. I'll call you later with more details. Love you, Lilly. Bye, baby!"

"Love you too, Mom."

But her mother hung up before she'd even finished the sentiment. Typical.

Her mother wasn't cruel, but the woman did tend to be a bit self-absorbed. She hadn't even asked how Lilly was. Not that she would have shared much with her mother. They didn't have that kind of relationship. They had more than some people did, and for that Lilly assured herself she was grateful. And on the plus side, she'd get to spend a little quality time with her mother when she came out for the wedding.

If you counted dress fittings and rehearsals as quality time.

A tiny sliver of sunlight peeked in through the long black curtains covering her window. The early-morning sounds of light traffic, barking dogs, and the faint peals of sirens in the distance filtered into her quiet room. No rest on the weekends in the city. Denver woke every day, a hub of activity, a rush of people off to enjoy the sights and pleasures of the city or escape into the peaceful, serene nature of the mountains. Or, for the non-nine-to-fivers, off to work.

Normally, her weekends were filled with the hectic rush of one or two weddings, but not this weekend. The only wedding they had in the next few weeks was Marie and Kenneth's. Still, Lilly did not do well with idle time, so she'd probably grab her calendar and some files and fit in a little work. They had plenty of upcoming weddings in the spring she could start on. Prep work to make the rush of April through June easier on them all. And no doubt her mother would be calling her much more often now that she'd agreed to help with the wedding. The woman had a single-minded focus she'd passed on to her daughter. But where Lilly used it for work, her mother used it for men.

She had started to rise from her bed when her phone rang again. Speaking of single-minded focus…

She pressed the phone to her ear with a sigh. "Mom, I told you I need to talk to Mo and Pru first—"

"I've been called a lot of things in my life, but 'mom' has never been one of them."

Lilly pulled the phone away from her ear at the deep voice, which sounded in no way like her soft-spoken mother. Crap! She'd answered without checking the caller. She'd simply assumed it was her mother calling back with more wedding requests.

She shoved Mo's voice out of her head, her roommate's oft-repeated immature joke playing in her brain at her embarrassing mistake.

"Oh, um, hello, Lincoln. I'm sorry; I was just talking to my mother and I thought she was calling back."

He chuckled, the warm rumbling sound causing a maelstrom of tingling awareness between her thighs.

"Nope. Just me, checking in to see how your morning is going, but now I'm wondering what you could possibly need to talk to your business partners about regarding your mother."

Still a little frazzled, her brain disconnected from her mouth, and she spewed out words without even thinking. "She's getting married again."

"Again?"

She heard no censure in his tone, no judgment. Merely simple curiosity. Perhaps that was why she chose to open up and discuss her personal life, something she rarely did with anyone. Or maybe it was because she hadn't had coffee yet and her brain wasn't fully awake. Or it could have something to do with this intense connection she and Lincoln had, one that started out physical and was quickly turning far too emotional for her comfort.

She was going with the coffee thing.

"Yes. This is her fourth—no, wait, her fifth marriage. Fourth wedding. I planned the last two, and she and her current fiancé would like me to plan this one as well."

"She asked you, her daughter, to plan her wedding?"

She could hear the shock in his voice, and, okay, maybe it was a bit unique to plan her own mother's wedding, but it was her profession.

"It's my job, Lincoln. I plan weddings."

"Yeah, for strangers. Clients. People who pay you."

Her mother would pay her. In fact, the one thing her mother did do was make sure her daughter was well compensated for her work. In her own stunted way, her mother overpaying Lilly was the woman's way of showing love. Vanessa Walsh could say the words all day long, but words only went so far. Actions spoke much louder. Sadly, her mother could only devote so much time to another person, and it was always saved for her latest love.

Never her daughter.

Money was nice, but Lilly could make her own money. She wanted time with her mom.

"Is her fiancé nice?"

"I have no idea. Much like my father, he's someone I've never met, but if he's anything like the last four of my mother's husbands, he'll be nice right up until he gets bored or things get too hard, then he'll hightail it out of town."

Did that sound a little cynical? She tried to root for her mother's happiness, she really did, but it was hard to believe in her mother's heart when the damn thing was so wishy-washy.

"I'm sorry, Lilly."

"It's no big deal."

His voice was low and soothing as it came over the line. "I think it is."

He was wrong. She'd stopped feeling sorry for herself long ago. As a child, she used to imagine her father was a spy, deep undercover. He left because there were dangerous mobsters after him and he had to protect her and her mother by disappearing. She used to stare out of her bedroom window in their tiny two-bedroom apartment and dream about him finally coming home, having put the bad guys in jail. Her mother could ditch her latest guy because Daddy was back! They'd be a family again and all live happily ever after.

But those were the silly wishes of a young girl. By the end of the fifth grade, real life had reared its ugly head and her mother was onto her second marriage. Lilly knew her father wasn't a spy, off saving the world and protecting her identity. He was just a man who knocked up his girlfriend and disappeared before his responsibilities could catch up to him. Meanwhile, her mother kept chasing love, always thinking she'd finally caught it and getting her heart stomped on.

Lilly didn't know what hurt worse: her mother's abandonment or watching the woman's heartbreaking sobs every time a guy left her.

"What about you?" She tried to inflect some cheer into her voice, anxious to change the subject away from her. "Are your parents still together?"

Lincoln paused. She held her breath, fearing he wouldn't let it go, but then he spoke.

"From the moment they met, my parents weren't apart more than a few days."

She could hear the smile in his voice as he spoke.

"Dad always said it was love at first sight, but Mom said he just wanted help on his math homework." He gave a soft laugh. "They married right out of high school. Dad was an electrician, and Mom was a mathematician. She was wicked smart with numbers. She even taught at Harvard as a guest professor for a few semesters. When I started getting into computers, she encouraged me, reminding me a lot of computing was math. We had fun figuring out programming and stuff together. Dad always said I got all my smarts from her, but I think I got the best of both of them. They were great parents."

The way he talked about his parents made her heart yearn. Growing up, she ached for a family dynamic like Lincoln was describing. It sounded so loving, so warm. But she also noticed a hint of sadness as he described his parents—and his use of the past tense.

"Were?"

He cleared his throat before he spoke again. "They passed away a little over five years ago. Mom had a stroke, and Dad just couldn't live without her. He died a few months later. The doctors said his heart just gave out."

"Oh, Lincoln." She placed a hand to her chest, feeling his loss as he spoke the words. "I'm sorry."

"Me, too. I miss them every day." He sighed, a wistful breath traveling over the airwaves. "They were both in their mid-seventies when they passed. I was a late-in-life baby. Mom had a few miscarriages early on, and they figured it just wasn't in the cards for them, but then I came along a couple years before Dad was set to retire. It was quite a shock for them."

"A happy shock, I'm sure."

He laughed softly. "Yeah. They always said I was their best surprise."

"They sound like they were amazing parents. I'm sure they would be proud of you, Lincoln."

"Careful, sweetheart," he said in a deep, warm tone. "Keep giving me compliments, and I might start to think you actually like me."

She was pretty sure she made that clear last night when she had inappropriate text sex with him.

"It doesn't matter what I think of you. We're completely unsuitable as a match in almost every way."

He chuckled. "There's the Lilly I know."

She joined in his laughter. "Seriously, Lincoln. I do think you are an amazing man. You're smart, funny, kind, sexy—"

"Why do I hear a *but* coming?"

"*But...*" She sighed. "I'm not sure we want the same things out of life, and you're still a part of a wedding party I'm running."

"Ah yes," he mused. "Your rule. Let's put that aside for a moment, considering it won't be an issue after next weekend."

Holy crap, he was right. Next weekend was Marie and Kenneth's wedding. The big obstacle getting in their way of pursuing something more, the thing she was holding onto like a lifeline, saving her from drowning in a sea of feelings for a man she already felt too much for, was rapidly approaching. Once the wedding was over, what was to stop them from being together? Nothing, really. So what the heck was she worrying about?

A lightbulb went off in her brain, illuminating the one situation she'd never pondered. What if—after the wedding, of course—she and Lincoln continued getting to know each other, and things actually worked out? Could she dare hope? Maybe they wouldn't be compatible enough to make it long term, but didn't she owe it to herself to try and find out? If Lincoln was willing to try and see, then why not? What the hell was holding her back?

Possible heartbreak.

Not if she led with her head and not her heart. She could do that. Right?

"We haven't really been on a proper date; we don't really know that much about each other or what we want in life. Do we?" Lincoln asked.

"I suppose you're right."

"Perfect! Then it's settled."

"What's settled?" She had no idea where his logic was going at the moment.

"After the wedding is over, I'm going to take you on a date, one where we keep our clothes on, and we'll get to know each other better. It doesn't have to be anything life-altering. We can just see where the night takes us, have a little fun."

His tone was slightly teasing, but the thought of going on an actual date with Lincoln made her want to squeal with joy and hide under the covers all at the same time.

"What do ya say, sweetheart?"

Honestly? She had no idea. Half of her was screaming *yes!* while the other half was busy planning a way to fake her own death and run far away from this man and the terrifying feelings he stirred in her.

"Uhhhhh."

"Why don't you think about it and get back to me later?" he asked, amusement coloring his voice.

She swallowed, finally finding her voice. "Yes. Thank you. I just need…to think about…things."

"Of course. But, Lilly," his smooth voice whispered in her ear over the phone, deep and resonant as if he were in the room, in her bed, holding her in his warm, safe arms. "While you're thinking about *things*, I'll be thinking about you. And about last night."

Chapter Thirteen

"Wow!" Lincoln stepped out of his car in front of the wedding venue. It was about a half an hour drive outside of the city in Genesee. No tall buildings or sidewalks here, nothing but a forest of dark green pines and stark leafless aspens. "This place is amazing."

This past week had been a rush of helping Marie and Kenneth get all the last-minute details in place. Max had been fully trained and assured his bosses he could handle the coffee shop for the next week while they were on their honeymoon. Lincoln had also promised them he'd check in and make sure everything was running smoothly. It was a small favor he would gladly perform in order to ensure his best friends could enjoy their special day and the start of their new life together as a married couple.

They sure as hell deserved it.

"Hey, man." Kenneth came strolling out of the huge log cabin Lincoln had just parked in front of. "Amazing, right?"

Lincoln stared up at the—well, it was a disservice to call the thing a simple cabin. This was no pioneer home, built to keep out the elements. This was a stunning display of craftsmanship. Architecture weaved into nature with a seamless beauty that both awed and inspired. The house loomed three stories high. Floor-to-ceiling windows covered the entire front of the structure, allowing natural light to pour in. The second floor sported a large wraparound deck where weddings took place in the summer months. Ken and Marie planned to have their ceremony inside. Good thing, too, because the wind had a bite to it.

Lincoln sniffed the air, the tip of his nose freezing slightly with the chill. It smelled damp, cold, like an impending snow.

"Don't even say it," Kenneth warned.

"What?"

"I saw you sniff." His friend glanced around, lowering his voice. "The weather report said a storm was coming in over the next forty-eight hours. I've managed to keep Marie from hearing about it, because if she hears snow is coming, she'll freak."

"How are you going to keep her from seeing the flakes when they fall down?" He pointed to the sky. "Because I'm pretty sure that's going to happen any moment now."

Kenneth looked up with a scowl, as if he could keep the snow from falling by sheer force of will.

"I'm hoping it'll hold off until after the wedding. It's less than twenty-four hours away. We might get lucky."

Lincoln laughed at his friend's optimism. "And you might get snowed in."

Kenneth glared at him. "Do you have to be such a pessimist?"

With a laugh, he held up his hands. "Hey, man. I'm simply being a realist."

"Yeah? Well, I'm *really* hoping it doesn't start snowing until after the wedding. A storm could ruin everything."

"Probably shouldn't have planned a wedding during one

of the snowiest months of the year, then."

Kenneth flipped him off. "It was the only time we could get all the family together, jerk."

He laughed, grabbing his overnight bag and tux from the car. "For Marie's sake, I will wish the snow to hold off."

"Thanks." The groom-to-be motioned to him. "Come on inside. I'll show you to our room and give you the lay of the place before the rehearsal starts."

He followed his friend inside, listening as the man explained about the rental Mile High Happiness had helped them secure. The eight-thousand-square-foot cabin was a full-service rental that boasted a full gourmet kitchen, a great room—where the wedding would be held—six bathrooms, eight bedrooms, and a sauna. Fancy digs.

"We'll drop off your stuff and head to the great room," Ken said as they entered the first floor, where half of the bedrooms and the kitchen were located. "Marie's already there with the Mile High Happiness women. The rehearsal is in a few hours, but I think they're doing some last-minute decorating or something."

His friends weren't the kind to freak out over things—they ran their own business; they knew how to deal with a crisis—but he sensed tension coming off Kenneth.

"Everything okay, man?"

Kenneth opened a door to the bedroom, glancing over his shoulder. "What? Oh, yeah. I just…I just want everything to be perfect for her." The man sighed. "She deserves the best."

Lincoln placed a comforting hand on his buddy's shoulder. "She's getting the best. She's getting you. That's all she cares about, I promise."

Kenneth shook his head. "You're wrong. She deserves better than me, but I'm not going to be stupid enough to tell her. I'm a lucky bastard, and I'll do everything in my power to make her happy for the rest of our lives."

He smiled. "Even threaten the weather?"

"Mother Nature better keep her precipitation locked up if she knows what's good for her."

He laughed, slapping Kenneth on the back as the men entered the room.

"Damn!" He let out a low whistle. "Is this a room or a suite?"

The large room boasted a huge bay window with a cushioned window seat that looked ideal for napping on a lazy Sunday. Two plush-looking high-back chairs sat in one corner, a coffee table in between them, while a dark red chaise longue took up the far wall. He spied an open door that appeared to lead to a private bathroom. The room rocked—except for one thing.

"Dude, is that the only bed?" He pointed to the large king taking up a significant portion of the back wall.

"Yes," Kenneth answered. "All the other rooms are filled with out-of-town guests. Marie wanted to bunk with her bridesmaids. Something about not sleeping together the night before the wedding being romantic. So you and I are bedmates." His friend pointed a finger at him. "And don't get any wild ideas. I'm a promised man. We can share like civilized adults, but no funny business."

Lincoln smiled. "I'm getting a weird flashback to sophomore year when we went to Key West for Spring Break and stayed in that awful rental."

Kenneth laughed. "Oh yeah! The one that said it had two beds, but it was one full and a pull-out sofa with no mattress. That sucked."

They'd shared the tiny bed for the night, scouring the small island until they found a hotel that had two beds with an opening the next morning. It had maxed out their credit cards, but it had been worth it. Two grown men sharing a full bed was not the most comfortable of situations.

"At least this is a king," he said with a shrug. There'd be much more room.

"And it's only for tonight. Everyone is leaving after the wedding tomorrow." A look of pure joy lit up Kenneth's face. "In twenty-four hours, Marie and I will be on our way to Cancún for our honeymoon."

His friend's happiness was infectious, and Lincoln found himself smiling. "I can't believe you and Marie are finally getting married."

Kenneth's jaw tightened, eyes misting over. "There was a time I thought this day might never come. When she was fighting for her—"

Lincoln wrapped an arm around his friend, pulling the guy in for a hug as the words clogged his throat.

"I know, man. But she's okay now. You guys are going to get married, live happily ever after, and be one of those annoying couples who make everyone jealous with their bliss."

He could attest to that firsthand.

"My goodness, the love abounds today," a soft voice spoke from the doorway. "I just left Marie hugging and happy crying with her bridesmaids. Don't witness too much of it with the menfolk, but it's great to see."

Lincoln pulled back to stare at the woman filling the bedroom doorway. The woman who'd been haunting his dreams for far too long, the woman who made him hard with nothing but a simple glance, the woman he hoped to have under him again the second this wedding was over.

"Hey, Lilly." Kenneth grinned. "Is it time to start the rehearsal?"

"Almost." She smiled at them both. "We're just waiting on a few more people, but if you guys want to head up now, that would be great."

Kenneth gave him a hard slap to the back before heading out of the room.

"Hey." He walked over to her, cupping her cheek. Her eyes darted to the side, checking for people who weren't there, before she leaned into his touch.

"Hi. Drive okay?"

"Mm-hmm." He stroked his thumb along the softness of her skin. Her eyes closed for a brief moment before they snapped open, emerald depths hazy with desire.

"We should get up there."

"Yeah, we should."

But neither of them made a move.

"There's a lot to do before the wedding." She leaned into him, face tilting up.

"Yup, a lot," he agreed, stepping closer until her breasts brushed against his chest.

"I have things to…"

Her words trailed off, eyes closing as she tilted her head up, lips parting. How could he refuse? He leaned down slightly. Not too far, because Lilly was a tall woman, the perfect height for him to brush his lips against hers. She moaned, the sound making him hard as granite. He grasped her hip, pulling her body flush against his as he deepened the kiss. She opened for him, greedily thrusting her tongue against his, devouring his lips with her own.

Damn! The woman was going to kill him.

Then, just as quickly, she was gone.

"Fuck."

He laughed at her curse. "I'd like to, but we have a rehearsal to get to."

She shook her head, smiling. "Ass. Come on, Romeo."

Adjusting his jeans, he followed her out of the room and up the stairs. He enjoyed the view as he watched the sway of her hips in her dark blue pencil skirt, the material hugging her curves with each rise of the steps. Noise filtered into his brain as they ascended to the main floor, which held the great room.

"Oh no!"

Marie's cry brought him out of his lust-induced stupor. Glancing at the large windows, he winced. Large, fat flakes fell from the sky, swirling to the ground in a beautiful yet ominous dance. He glanced around the room, focusing on Marie, who stood in the center, staring straight out the window, Kenneth behind her, holding her in his arms.

"At least it's pretty?" Lincoln heard his friend say.

"It's beautiful, babe, but now the roads are going to be a nightmare." Marie turned, burying her head in Kenneth's chest. "What if people can't make it up?"

The heartbroken voice, muffled by his friend's chest, struck a chord in Lincoln. This wasn't fair. Marie and Ken were an amazing couple. Too much of life had tried to mess with them. They deserved to have one day free of disaster. He wanted to help, but he had no idea what to do.

"Marie." Lilly made her way over to the forlorn bride-to-be. "Everything will be okay."

"But it's snowing!"

The wedding planner smiled. "Yes, I can see, but Colorado is used to February snow. You've lived here long enough to know that, right?" Marie nodded. "Don't you worry about a thing. Let me makes some calls and see what I can do."

He hurried to his friend's side as he watched Lilly pull out her phone and speak in hushed tones to whoever was on the other end of the line.

"Okay, everyone." Mo—sporting purple stripes in her blond hair—called everyone over to the center of the room. "While Lilly works her magic, why don't we go over what's going to happen tomorrow? We want to do two run-throughs so we get everything down pat for the big day."

Everyone gathered at the small woman's command. He lined up next to Rachel, half his concentration on the woman standing off to the side of the room, pacing as she spoke on the phone. He had no idea who Lilly was calling or what she was trying to orchestrate, but he'd bet his hard drive if anyone could push the weather back to make this wedding perfect, it would be her.

They ran through the motions of the rehearsal twice—easy enough to walk down an aisle and stand there—as the snow continued to fall outside the windows. The majestic sight added both beauty and worry to the proceedings. Once the rehearsal was completed, everyone was dismissed. Mo announced the rehearsal dinner would be in an hour, downstairs in the large dining area. Kenneth's parents had talked about using a restaurant in the area but decided to hire the staff of the wedding to prepare and serve the rehearsal dinner after all.

Everyone headed to their rooms save for him, Marie, and Kenneth. He stood with his friends, a solid presence behind them as they anxiously waited for Lilly to get off the phone. He had no idea what she'd done, but judging by the satisfied grin on her face, he'd bet she just pulled off a miracle for his best friends. Every time he thought this woman had impressed the hell out of him, she went and one-upped it.

"Fantastic. Consider the favor repaid. Thanks, Twyla." Lilly smiled, slipped her phone into the pocket of her skirt, and headed their way. "I have great news."

"You got Boreas to agree to tone it down a bit?"

Everyone stared at Marie. The woman shrugged.

"He's the Greek God of winter." At their continued silence, she threw up her hands. "Geesh, no one appreciates a history minor."

"I do, babe." Kenneth kissed her cheek. "Nerds are hot."

She elbowed him gently but smiled. "Damn right we are."

Lilly motioned to the snow outside. "The snow is making the roads slick and icy, but I called in a favor with a limo company. They agreed to meet the vendors who aren't here yet and the guests who will be arriving tomorrow at their business and drive everyone up and back."

Marie let out a high-pitched shriek. "Lilly, you are the absolute best!"

The woman flung her arms around the wedding planner. Lincoln held back a snort of laughter at the panicked look on Lilly's face as the woman tried to gently pat his friend's back and extricate herself from the hug.

"I'm simply here to make sure your special day runs smoothly."

He called bullshit on that. Lilly went above and beyond for her clients. And from what he learned of her the other day, that giving extended into her personal life. Sure, her mom might be paying her to organize her latest wedding, but he knew Lilly would have done it no matter what. The woman might try to hide behind a wall of propriety and ice, but inside she was a big ol' softie who just wanted the people around her to be happy.

Damn, she was amazing.

"Oh." Marie sniffed, wiping at her eyes with the back of her hand. "Now I have to fix my makeup."

"You look amazing," Lilly said with a shake of her head.

"You do, babe, but I can take you to your room if you want to freshen up before dinner."

"Yes, I think that would be for the best. Thank you, Lilly."

"Just doing my job."

He watched as his friends headed upstairs to where he assumed Marie was staying. Lilly stood, watching them go with a longing smile on her face. He could relate. His friends had the kind of relationship people dreamed about. The kind you only read about in books or saw in movies. There'd been many a time over the years he'd compared his own failed marriage to his friends' relationship and wondered where he went wrong. Fair? No, but hard not to do.

"Admit it," he said as he stepped up to her side. "You're some kind of superhero, aren't you?"

She laughed, her eyes still on the spot where Marie and Kenneth had disappeared. "Not a superhero. Just really good at my job."

"Really good at making people happy."

"I like making people happy." She sighed. "The world needs more happy."

"And what about you?"

She turned to face him. "What about me?"

"What would make you happy?"

Her gaze traced over him, eyes heating, waking up every cell in his body. It took all his willpower to hold still when what he really wanted to do was haul her into him and worship every single inch of her body with his tongue.

"You." The word whispered out of her of its own volition.

"That can be arranged, sweetheart." His voice was so low and husky he almost didn't recognize it.

"You're still a client." She shrugged. "Sort of."

He lifted a brow, clenching his hands into fists to keep from reaching out to touch her. "Not after tomorrow at five, I'm not."

A cheeky grin tilted her lips. "Technically, the wedding ends at ten."

He couldn't help it—he threw his head back and laughed. "Okay, you win. Ten. But after ten…"

She bit her lip. He wanted nothing more than to soothe the small pain with his tongue.

"Tomorrow." The word whispered out of her. "The place

is booked until Sunday. Mo and I usually hang around to make sure the place is all cleaned up, so if you want to stay after the wedding, we can…"

His eyes widened in shock. "Seriously?" They'd been talking, flirting, even gotten a little naughty over the phone, but he was still surprised she'd finally agreed.

She nodded. "*After* the wedding."

"After," he agreed.

"Now let's hurry up. There's a rehearsal dinner to get to." She winked, heading down the stairs.

It took a moment for his brain and body to catch up. Tomorrow. After the wedding, he would be with Lilly Walsh again. His body vibrated with such a fierce need he almost couldn't take it. Just over twenty-four hours. Didn't seem like much in the long run, but right now…he feared waiting for Lilly would be the longest day of his life.

Chapter Fourteen

Wedding days were normally times of exhilaration for Lilly. The big day arrived, and all the work she'd put in with her couples came to fruition. She never stressed because she always had a plan for each and every emergency that could present itself. Over the years, she had seen everything from exes showing up to try and object to the wedding to out-of-control drunk in-laws losing their clothing on the dance floor.

Each instance had been met with Lilly's firm yet polite guidance of the situations. Whatever it called for—coffee and a quiet room, the adorable distraction of a flower girl/ring bearer dance, or, in one case, a call to Denver PD—Lilly could handle it. She had nerves of damn steel.

So why was her stomach currently filled with a million anxious butterflies?

She glanced across the vast great room. The chairs had all been set, the aisle runner laid, and sweet smells of the fresh-cut flowers filled the room. Standing at the center, directly in front of the floor-to-ceiling windows, stood a dark oak arch covered in beautiful white gardenias and pale purple peonies. Normally, the arch would be used outside on the large deck for a wedding, but since it was still snowing, they had it indoors.

Yesterday, the limo service had picked up all the incoming out-of-town guests and supplies and driven up the snowy I-70 pass from Denver to Genesee. Marie and Kenneth had been extremely relieved, thanking her and Mo a million times before the night was over. Not necessary. It was her job to make sure nothing ruined her clients' perfect day. Not even Mother Nature.

The bridal party was currently getting ready, the caterer prepping the meal, the band warming up. Everything looked to be in order.

So what was with this terrified twitch in her stomach?

"Wow, Lilly. The place looks amazing."

She turned to face the very source of her disquiet. Lincoln strode into the great room, head swiveling this way and that as he took in all the changes she and Mo had spent hours setting up. Though it didn't take much to make this place awe-inspiring. The large house—mansion, really—had been built by a famous architect whose wife always wanted a luxury cabin in the woods. He came out to Colorado and built her this castle masquerading as a cabin, but after one Rocky Mountain winter, the wife had refused to step foot in the state again.

Her loss. Genesee's gain.

The architect donated the building to the city, a beautiful rental property to drive income into the small city's coffer and a nice tax write-off for him. And lucky for her, the city liked to rent it out for big events like weddings. They'd used this location half a dozen times before, but she never got tired of staying there. The view from these windows was majestic—a large wooded forest off to one side, the sparkling lights of Denver off to the other—and the massive pine ceiling beams made the entire place smell like the woods after a fresh rain.

If someone ever built her a place like this, she'd never leave.

"Thank you," she said to the man who couldn't build her a cabin castle but probably could build her a new computer she wouldn't want to toss into the wall every other day.

"Marie and Kenneth are gonna flip." His eyes settled on her, a grin brightening his handsome face.

"It's my job to make sure everything is beautiful for their big day, but I'm sure they'll be too busy staring at each other to notice. As they should be."

He nodded. "As they should be."

His gaze roamed over her, eyes lighting with a different kind of appreciation than the one he gave the room.

"You look beautiful."

Heat rose on her cheeks. She glanced down to her standard uniform when running a wedding, her trusty LBD and low-heeled black pumps. The black dress was modest but fancy enough for any level of formal event. The scalloped neckline hit right below her collarbone, edging out to her shoulders, where the three-quarter sleeves of the dress allowed for style and comfort. The skirt flared out at her waist, hitting just below her knees to allow ease of movement in case she had to hurry to put out a fire. She supposed it was a beautiful dress, but she'd never felt beautiful in it. She wore it for purpose, not pleasure.

Yet the way Lincoln stared at her, devouring her with his eyes, made her wonder if the dress would be considered work appropriate had she not been in her current profession.

"Thank you, I—" She paused with a frown. "Where's your tux?"

For the first time since he entered the room, Lilly noticed Lincoln's attire. The man had on a ratty pair of jeans and a dark green long-sleeved shirt, which set off the flecks of gold in his hazel gaze. Perfect eye-popping sweater or not, it wasn't proper wedding attire.

"In my room."

She huffed at his nonchalance. "Shouldn't you be getting ready? The wedding is in"—she glanced at the watch attached to her clipboard—"two hours."

He smiled, a soft chuckle escaping those delicious lips. "I'm a guy. We don't need two hours to put clothes on."

Stupid fashion industry. Lilly could admit she had a thing for stylish clothes and designer shoes, but it pissed her off the way guys could put on an outfit without a thought and women had to match style, pattern, color. They had to wear layers because God forbid they make any type of top or dress that wasn't constructed of such sheer fabric your bra and panties showed with even the barest of backlighting.

"Okay, but don't you have to do other things?"

He arched a brow. "Like what?"

"Wash up, manly bonding time?" She gestured vaguely at his face. "Shave?"

A large palm came up to scrape against the scruffiness on his jaw. The sound hit her ears, causing every inch of her body to come alive with need. Oh hell, this was going to be the longest wedding ever.

"You don't like my beard?"

It wasn't much of one. More like nicely trimmed scruff. She lived in Denver, hipster central. She'd seen men who could braid their beards, men who hung Christmas bulbs in their beards—once a guy even had a tiny lizard sitting in his nest of a beard. That was a weird one. Even for Denver.

"It doesn't matter what I like. It's about what Kenneth and Marie want for their day."

His lips split in a wide, knowing grin. "So you do like my beard?"

His eyebrows bobbed, but she chose to ignore him,

focusing intently on her clipboard even though she'd double-checked everything on her list.

Lincoln threw his head back and laughed, the sound booming out of him, echoing in the large, high-ceiling room.

"Not to worry, Ms. Walsh. Marie and Kenneth gave me the all clear for the beard. They don't care what I look like as long as I'm here, and I'm currently *right here* because Ken is having his pre-wedding freak-out shower. Which means he's taking a long, very cold shower to calm his nerves while singing every Strokes song at the top of his lungs. Badly." He stuck a finger in his ear and wiggled. "I had to escape for fear my eardrums would burst and I wouldn't hear my cue to walk down the aisle."

She laughed, covering her mouth with her hand as she realized she was laughing about her client stressing when it was her job to make sure he didn't.

"Oh no." She removed her hand, unable to wipe the smile from her face. "Is he okay? Does he need anything?"

Lincoln shrugged. "Just to marry the love of his life. I can't tell who's more excited for today, Kenneth or Marie. I think if it weren't for their families insisting on celebrating this joyous occasion, they would have run off to the courthouse the minute Marie said yes. Kenneth said he can't wait to start their forever."

"The best kind of love feels that way." At his curious stare, she shrugged. "Or so I've heard."

He watched her for a long moment, gaze contemplative. She shifted under his scrutiny, wishing she knew what was going on in his mind. What had put that odd look on his face?

"You ever been in love, Lilly?"

Crap! The problem with having a job revolving around love and happily ever afters was everyone eventually asked her if she had experienced love. While she'd had a few boyfriends she cared for and one disaster of a relationship where she discovered she was the other woman—hello, shame and humiliation—she'd never truly been in love. Because she didn't really believe in love—at least, not for her. Something she could never tell anyone associated with her business.

Lincoln stood there, hazel eyes staring deep into hers, as if he could see her soul. Pick out every lie, every misdeed. But not to judge; no, Lincoln wasn't like that. He liked to solve problems. She guessed as a computer guy that was kind of *his* job. But she wasn't his problem to figure out.

"No." She kept it simple, turning the question around to get the pressure off her. "How about you? Ever been in love?"

His eyes shuttered, face going blank as he shut down all emotion. He turned to stare out the window with a clenched jaw. He was silent so long she thought he might not answer, but then he said, "I thought I was. Once. But it turned out to be nothing even close to that."

His expression might not give anything away, but she could hear the hurt in his voice. The anger. Whatever happened to Lincoln obviously caused him pain, and she ached for him.

"I'm sorry."

She reached out to touch his arm, but suddenly he came alive, turning to her with a falsely bright smile plastered on his face. She'd gotten to know the man fairly well over the past few weeks, and he was genuine through and through. But not now. Not this smile. It wasn't a happy one, but one that was meant to cover up his real feelings, to close a subject. A subject he started, she might point out.

"I better get back to the anxious groom. Any more cold water and he might be too shriveled up to perform his husbandly duties tonight." He bobbed his brow.

Knowing better than to push a subject neither of them seemed all that eager to discuss, she rolled her eyes. "Classy, Lincoln. Very classy."

"Hey, I'm a classy guy." He leaned in with a grin, his lips brushing against her ear as he whispered, "If I wasn't, I'd tell you how absolutely fuckable you look in that dress."

She felt the barest brush of his lips against the sensitive spot on her neck just below her ear. A shiver of anticipation ran up her spine. After tonight, he'd no longer be off-limits. Could she really do this? Start a sexual relationship with a man she knew wasn't a good match for her? Let her body take control and keep her heart out of it?

His tongue came out to gently stroke along her pulse point as his teeth closed down with a sharp, tiny love bite. Her knees weakened, all the blood rushing between her legs at the sensual move.

Yes. Yes, she most certainly could.

...

Lincoln wiped his face with the back of his hand, brushing away a few stray tears as he watched his two best friends kiss for the first time as man and wife. He wasn't ashamed at the release of emotions. Real men cried, and that toxic masculinity bullshit could shove it. The two people he loved most in the world just got something they feared they would never have a few short years ago.

A future together.

He cried when Marie got sick and they all feared they might lose her, and he would damn well cry now. Happy tears, of course. Damn, he was so over the moon for them. As they walked back down the aisle, arm in arm, man and wife, he couldn't stop the huge grin from taking over his face. Kenneth's cousin had to nudge him to remind him they were still in wedding mode and Rachel was waiting for him to escort her down the aisle.

"Wasn't it a beautiful ceremony?" She sniffed, dabbing at

her eyes with a tissue as she linked arms with him.

"Yeah. And now comes the best part. Cake."

She laughed as they made their way down the aisle, smiling at all the people who clapped at Kenneth and Marie's exit. It had been a beautiful ceremony. Short, too, which made it even better. And now they'd get to the fun stuff: food, drinks, dancing, and then...truth be told, as happy as Lincoln was for his friends, now that the official ceremony was over, his happiness had turned into excitement. For after—for tonight.

The second those two left for their honeymoon, he'd be free. No longer attached to any client of Lilly's, no longer bound by her rule. After tonight they wouldn't be wedding planner and best man anymore. They'd simply be Lilly and Lincoln. Two people who shared an amazing night—and text exchange—once and, if luck was with him, would share again. Many times over.

"Hey, everyone." Lilly's partner Mo popped up at the end of the aisle and ushered the wedding party over. "Lilly is taking Kenneth and Marie outside to do some winter shots with the photographer. We're going to let everyone pile out of here and head into the library for drinks and hors d'oeuvres. While the waitstaff is setting up the tables, the photographer will come back for the group shots, so if you have to use the facilities, do it now."

The parents headed toward the restroom, along with the ringbearer and the other groomsman, leaving only Lincoln, the bridesmaids—who were off to the side checking one another's hair and dresses—and Mo.

"You looked good up there, Lincoln."

"Oh, um, thank you."

She chuckled. "You're welcome, but I wasn't the one who said it."

She glanced out the window. He followed her gaze to see

Lilly draping a pale lavender cloak over Marie's shoulder as the snow fell down around the couple. They looked like they were in a snow globe. Beautiful. But not as beautiful as the woman who wore a simple black coat, clipboard in hand as she positioned the couple then hurried out of the shot for the photographer to capture the stunning moment.

"It was unconsciously whispered in my ear as you walked down the aisle."

He turned his attention back to Mo, who tapped the small, black headset she wore.

"In fact, I believe the exact words were 'sonofabitch, he looks damn edible in a tux.'" The woman winked.

Fantastic. He was already having enough trouble waiting for tonight. How the hell was he supposed to get through the entire reception knowing the woman he craved wanted to eat him up?

"Better start reciting times tables if you don't want these pictures to be NSFW."

He glanced at Mo in question. When the woman's eyes darted to his crotch, he quickly adjusted himself as discreetly as possible. Yeah, even thinking of Lilly got him ready to go, but since he was pretty sure Marie would kick his ass if he was sporting wood in her wedding pictures, he did as Mo suggested and started some complex math equations in his head. It worked, and soon the happy couple was back inside, noses lightly red from the cold but happy smiles still firmly affixed.

They quickly ran through the preset list of photos as the catering company set up the great room for the reception. It amazed him how quickly everyone worked. Within fifteen minutes, the guests came back in and everyone sat for dinner. Lilly grabbed the mic and welcomed Mr. and Mrs. Buller for the first time. Everyone cheered, clinking their glasses until the happy couple kissed.

The reception went off without a hitch. Lilly seamlessly moved each portion of the night into the next with a practiced ease he found impressive and sexy as hell. Rachel gave a touching speech that made everyone tear up. He went for the jokes in his speech but couldn't let it end without putting some real emotion into an event they all feared might never come. By the time he sat back down, there wasn't a dry eye in the room, his included.

After a delicious dinner and some equally delectable cake came the dancing portion of the evening. He had to admit, he was having fun, but every time his gaze fell on Lilly, every time she spoke, his mind raced ahead to later tonight.

Would she come to his room? Was he supposed to go to hers? She'd told him to stay, but she hadn't mentioned where to meet. They hadn't really discussed anything beyond her desire to be with him again. He sure as hell wanted to be with her.

Finally, all the food had been consumed, all the traditions carried out, and they were tossing birdseed as Marie and Kenneth carefully hurried down the front walk to their waiting limo. A small pang of sadness hit him directly in the chest as he watched his two closest friends go into the night to catch their honeymoon flight, off to start their new life together.

You sap, you live below them. Not much is going to change.

Yeah, nothing would really change, but in a way, everything would. He'd been married before. He knew the drill.

People started to head to their cars and the other stretch limos Lilly had arranged to pick up the guests they'd dropped off earlier. Before long, Lincoln turned and headed inside. The rest of the bridal party was either already gone or packing up to leave. The caterers and staff were cleaning up, putting away all the magic of the evening.

No.

There was one bit left. The most magical part of the entire night. She stood before the large windows, backlit by a bright, full moon. Doling out orders left and right. In charge and sexy as hell. Dark brown hair coiled into a low bun, dress fitting her body like a glove, those damn sexy glasses slipping down her nose, begging him to slide them off her face as he kissed her senseless.

Lilly turned, spying him. She bit her lip, eyes heating even from all the way across the room. He glanced at the clock and held up a finger while mouthing, "My room? One hour?"

She nodded, a small smile curling her red lips.

One more hour. Just one more hour until heaven. Until Lilly.

Chapter Fifteen

Lilly stared at the timepiece on her clipboard. Forty-five minutes had passed since Lincoln silently mouthed those four words that had no business being erotic but had revved her engine quicker than anything ever had before.

My room. One hour.

They'd agreed to see where this thing was headed after the wedding, and now the time had come. But even though the bride and groom were en route to their tropical honeymoon, the guests headed off to their respective homes, and the caterer had packed up the last of their supplies, she still had work to do. The rental had to be as pristine as when they'd first arrived, and while they had a great company coming in tomorrow for a deep cleaning, she liked to do a final walkthrough. Just to make sure nothing had been left behind or seriously damaged.

Normally, it was her favorite part of the night. The high of surveying the end of a job well done. All the planning and stress behind her. The happy clients off to their new lives as spouses. But not this time, not tonight. Tonight she was edgy, anxious...okay, she was horny. But could anyone blame her? She had the sweet and sexy Lincoln Reid waiting just a floor below to take care of her every carnal desire.

And boy, would he. She knew from experience just how attentive he could be. Memories assailed her mind, along with some new ideas she hoped he'd be game for. She had no idea what would happen after tonight. He mentioned something about a date. Did that mean he saw them as a longer-term thing? And if so, what did that mean for her and her list?

Honestly, the more she got to know Lincoln, the sillier her list seemed. Her mother might jump into relationships headfirst with her eyes clouded by emotions, but Lilly could see clearly.

80 percent clear.

Maybe seventy-five.

Twenty when he was naked.

The point was, she wasn't all emotion in this situation. Her brain had some say. Hopefully enough to protect her heart if everything went sideways.

"Hey, Lil." Mo slid up beside her. "I can handle the last walkthrough if you want to get out of here."

She glanced over at her roommate's knowing grin. No matter how eager she was to get down and dirty with Lincoln again, she had a job to do, and she wouldn't eschew that for him. Or any man.

"You don't need to do that. I'm almost done, anyway."

Mo lost her pleasant smile, exasperation coloring her face. "Oh my God, just go do him already!"

Her head snapped up, glasses slipping down her nose. She pushed them back up with a single finger, staring at her friend. "Excuse me?"

"Lincoln." Mo's lips curved again. "I know he's downstairs waiting for you to rock his world."

"That is the most ridiculous thing I have ever heard,

Moira. How on earth could you possibly know a thing like that?"

Mo tossed her purple-streaked hair back and laughed. "Oh please, everyone within five miles of you two can feel the fire."

"That doesn't mean—"

"One." The woman held up a hand, counting off on her fingers. "You slept with him before, and I know it was good because you blush every time his name is mentioned."

She did not!

"Two, he totally has a thing for you."

Though she hated to give her roommate any fodder, she couldn't help but ask, "He does?"

Mo laughed. "Yup. The man's got serious puppy dog eyes where you're concerned."

And that was a good thing? She wouldn't know, having never had a dog herself.

"Three," Mo continued. "His car is still out front, so I know he hasn't left yet."

"Maybe he's still packing up," she countered.

Mo shook her head. "And four, I saw him say 'my room one hour' fifty minutes ago."

Damn Mo and her twenty-twenty vision.

"Look." Mo tucked an arm around Lilly's waist, gently pulling the clipboard from her hands. "The place is rented out until tomorrow. The cleaning company isn't coming until noon. I'm heading out soon, and I assume you have a ride home with Lincoln after you ride his—"

Lilly smashed her hand over her friend's mouth, embarrassment heating her cheeks. "Mo!"

Mo waggled her eyebrows, and Lilly couldn't stop the small chuckle from escaping her lips.

"Yes, Lincoln can drive me home. I'll stay to make sure everything is set for the cleaning crew. You can head home tonight."

Mo nodded. "Then by my count, you have ten minutes to freshen up or do whatever you need to do before heading to his room and letting that man worship you like the goddess you are."

She grinned. "Maybe I should take fifteen minutes. Make him sweat a little."

Mo shrugged. "Goddesses are rarely on time."

"Thanks, Mo." She gave her friend a quick squeeze.

"Anytime, hun. Now go get some!"

The command was amplified by a sharp smack to her backside. She cursed, rubbing her smarting bottom and glaring at Mo over her shoulder. Her friend's laughter followed her as she made her way down the stairs. She didn't need to change clothes or make the man wait any longer. *She* couldn't wait any longer. The anticipation over the past twenty-four hours was likely to kill her.

Death by lust. Terrible way to go.

As she reached Lincoln's door, she hesitated. If she knocked, there would be no going back. She had no idea why she was so nervous. It wasn't like they hadn't done this before.

Yeah, but we were strangers.

Two people simply seeking solace in the physical connection. It wouldn't be like that tonight. It'd be hot and amazing, she was certain, but they knew each other now. More than she'd like to admit. It wasn't just physical tonight. Emotions would be involved. She still wasn't sure how she felt about that.

Now or never.

She raised her hand to knock, but the door swung open. Lincoln stood there with a devilish grin, hands braced on the doorframe above his head. He wore nothing but his tux pants, unbuttoned and hanging low on his hips. His lean frame caught her eye, captivating her with all the sharp planes and dips she wanted to explore. With her tongue.

"Hey, beautiful."

"Hi." She adjusted her glasses even though they sat perfectly on her nose. "Can I come in?"

He stepped back, motioning for her to enter. She stepped inside his room, noticing how different it was from hers. She and Mo had stayed on the third floor in a small but nice bedroom with two twin beds. This room, however, was quite large and would feel larger if not for the massive king-size bed taking up most of the floor space. She was eternally grateful he'd suggested his room tonight. With their combined tall statures, she doubted their, um, activities would be comfortable in a twin.

"So." She wandered about the room, wiping her sweaty palms on her skirt. "The ceremony was nice."

"It was fantastic. You did an amazing job, Lilly."

A flush rose on her face. "Mo and Pru helped." They were a team, and she could always count on her friends and business partners to have her back.

"True." Lincoln nodded. "Still, you are amazing, and I know Marie and Kenneth loved their day. Everything went off without a hitch, from the emergency snow transportation to the bouquet toss to the farewell birdseed. You're like a wedding planning superhero. With two left feet."

She laughed softly. "I warned you I couldn't dance."

He lifted a finger, crooking it at her in a "come here" motion. Since that's exactly where she wanted to be, she obliged. The moment she got close enough, he snagged her around the waist, pulling her into him. He buried his face in her neck as his other hand came up to pull the functional but classy jeweled clip from her hair.

The strands came tumbling down from the updo she had them in, kinking around her shoulders because of all the product she'd used to keep her hair in place. Why couldn't it fall gracefully around her shoulders like it did in the movies? Lincoln didn't seem to care. He gently tossed the clip onto one of the large chairs facing the curtain-drawn window. His large hand came up to cradle the back of her head.

"I have to tell you, sweetheart, it was damn hard getting through tonight without sporting wood."

She snorted. "Charming."

"I never claimed to be a gentleman." His gaze roamed over her. "Every time I saw you, every time I even thought of you, of this moment right here, my body tightened with anticipation."

Since she felt exactly the same way, she didn't chide him for it.

"Lincoln," she whispered, finding it hard to drag enough air into her lungs to form words. "Did you bring condoms?"

She had but left them upstairs. The last thing she wanted to do right now was climb two flights of stairs for protection.

His head swiveled to the bedside table, where a box of condoms lay open, a strip out and waiting.

"I love a man who comes prepared."

"Sweetheart, with you, I plan to come all night." The hand cupping her waist slid down her hip to curve around her thigh, under the skirt of her dress. "But you first."

She moaned, loud and long as his fingers gently caressed her inner thigh, going higher until he found the silk of her panties, already damp for him. He made a low growling sound in his throat, rubbing her just where she needed. Well, almost.

"Lincoln, I need more."

"What, sweetheart? Tell me what you need."

"You," she panted. "Inside me."

His lips pressed a hungry kiss to hers as his fingers delved under the scrap of silk. She opened her mouth on a gasp, and he thrust his tongue inside. She eagerly met him, tasting the sweetness of his lips as he pressed one long finger inside her. It astounded her how well this man knew her body. She was fully clothed, he was partially clothed, and she was minutes away from orgasm. He added a second finger, pressing the heel of his palm to her center.

Make that seconds away.

She ripped her mouth from his, arms coming up to clutch his shoulders as her knees locked, the pressure building up inside her.

"Lincoln, I'm…"

"Let go," he whispered in her ear. "I'm right here."

He quickened his pace, mouth latching onto her neck, sucking and biting gently. The pressure was too much, and she soon found herself cresting a wave of pleasure so intense her legs gave out. Thankfully, Lincoln tightened the arm he had around her waist, catching her as she melted into a puddle of sated goo.

"Hot damn, Lilly. You are the sexiest woman I have ever known."

She graced him with a small smile, the only muscle she could control at the moment. "Take me to bed, Lincoln." Because she was in no way done with him. Not by a long shot.

"Yes, ma'am."

He moved his hand, pulling her panties off as he left her and scooping under her knees to carry her to the bed. She sat there as he carefully unzipped her dress, peeling the garment from her slowly, with a gentleness that made moisture gather in her eyes. She blinked it away. Now was not the time for blubbery emotions. She knew for a fact a night with Lincoln included multiple orgasms, and she intended to enjoy each and every one.

"You seem to be overdressed," she stated when he finally removed her dress, laying her back and sitting on his heels above her, staring.

"What? Oh, I, um, you're not wearing a bra."

His befuddlement amused her. No, she hadn't been wearing anything but silk panties under her dress. "The dress has a built-in bra. Easier for formal occasions."

"And bedroom occasions." He waggled his eyebrows.

She laughed, her hands going to the button on his pants. "Now you."

He placed a hand over hers, stopping her exploration. "Wait."

For what? They were just getting to the good part. The good*er* part, anyway.

"Why?"

He grinned, his gaze roaming over her body, tightening her nipples, making her ache as fire lit their hazel depths.

He shook his head, moving down the bed until he was at the very end. "I'm not done worshipping you yet."

Far be it from her to deny a man his adoration.

He lifted one ankle, kissing the arch of her foot, continuing to caress her skin with his lips as he moved from her ankle to her calf, up to her thigh, to graze along her hip, and then, finally, placing her leg over his shoulder, his mouth descended on the very part of her that craved him the most.

"Lincoln!" she cried out as he thrust his tongue against her, sucking and working her into such a frenzy she bucked her hips against his face.

Normally, she'd be embarrassed, but she was too far gone to care. Too lost in the rapture of his worship. Much sooner than she would have guessed, she felt her body tighten again. A whimper sounded in the air, and she realized it came from her.

"I've got you."

Lincoln's deep voice seemed to come out of a fog of lust and need. She felt his hand join his mouth, fingers pressing into her once again at just the right moment, causing her to cry out with a release that rocked her entire being.

"Oh my God, I don't think anything could be better than that."

His lips curled in a smug smile as he crawled up her body. "Wanna bet?"

She grinned, wrapping her arms around his neck. "Lose the pants and let's find out."

He stared at her a moment, finger coming out to trace the frames of her glasses. "These are sexy as hell."

"Yeah?"

"I'll admit to a few teacher and secretary fantasies about them."

She snorted. "Such a guy."

"Guilty." He pinched the frames between his thumb and pointer finger. "Do you need them, or can I take them off?"

Since the last time they'd been together she'd been wearing her contacts and seen every glorious inch of him, she nodded. "You can take them off."

He removed her glasses, setting them carefully on the bedside table. She blinked, his blurry face coming into slight focus. She had really bad eyesight. Lucky for her, she didn't need to see much for what came next.

"The pants. Lose them."

He laughed. "Anything you say."

Ooooh, she liked the sound of that.

Lincoln rose from the bed, shucking his pants and boxers off in one rapid move. She stared in awe as his cock bobbed up and down, finally free of the confines of the material. Reaching out, she grasped the hard, velvety appendage, stroking her hand up and down, reveling in the feel of him.

"Careful, Lilly. Much more of that and I'll embarrass myself."

"Really?" She found that lack of control hard to believe.

His eyes stared down at her, serious and full of emotion.

"I haven't been with anyone since you. I haven't wanted anyone else since you."

She paused in her stroking, swallowing past the lump of emotion in her throat. His confession caught her off guard. The raw vulnerability of what he'd just revealed humbled her, and she couldn't lie to him. Not now. Not after that.

"Me either." She cleared her throat as the words stuck. "I haven't been with anyone since you either."

A happy smile lit his face. He reached over to grab one of the foil packets on the bedside table. "Well then, should we—"

"Yes!"

She grabbed the condom packet from his hand, eager to put this back in the physical realm. He laughed as she tore open the foil, but his laughter died when she rolled the latex down his length, ending in a groan as she squeezed the base of him.

"Lilly."

She reached up, grabbing his biceps and pulling him down to her. "I want you, Lincoln, now."

"Yes," he growled. "Now."

Settling himself between her thighs, he positioned himself at her entrance and thrust. They both cried out in unison as he entered her. She clutched his back, nails digging in. She wasn't even sorry for the marks she might be leaving, because he was sure as hell leaving marks on her heart. Only fair she should mark his body.

"Damn, Lilly. You feel even more amazing than I remember."

"You, too," she panted. "Move, Lincoln."

He complied with her demand, thrusting his hips in a slow, torturous rhythm.

"Faster." She wasn't going to last long. Unbelievable, since she'd come to completion twice already, but with this man, all bets were off. "Harder!"

He quickened his pace, slamming into her with a force that made her eyes cross and her body tighten. No matter what she demanded, this man followed through. He listened, he fulfilled, he astounded.

She thrust her hands into his hair, pulling at the short strands, tugging him down so she could capture his lips with her own. The connection of their bodies on every level was too much. Before long, she found herself cresting a wave of pleasure so intense it brought tears to her eyes. She tore her mouth away from his to cry out his name as she felt her body explode with euphoria unlike anything she'd ever experienced before.

"Lilly!"

Her own name pierced through the fog of bliss, shouted from the lips of a man who surprised her at every turn.

They collapsed, breaths heaving out of their chests, sweat drenching their bodies. Lincoln moved to his side, pulling her on top of him. As he slipped from her body, she felt the loss in more than one way.

"Well," she sucked in a deep breath, trying to lighten the heavy mood she felt welling up inside her chest. "I'd say that was a success."

He laughed softly. "Don't you mean sexcess?"

She snorted.

Smart, sexy, kind, and funny. That tiny voice in the back of her head that had been whispering she couldn't separate sex from her feelings had gone from a dim hum to a shrill warning bell.

Oh crap, she was in trouble. Big time.

Chapter Sixteen

Once again, Lilly found herself waking from the most restful sleep she'd had since...since the last time she slept with Lincoln. The guy was like her very own homeopathic sleep aid. Hmmm, how would one market that? *Take three Reid orgasms and get the most restful sleep of your life. Side effects may include a dependency on sex, fantasies about computer nerds, and catching feelings.* Because as much as she'd like to deny it, she hadn't awakened with just a sated and well-rested body. She also feared this tugging feeling in her chest was a suspicious case of the cares.

Before they went any further, they really needed to sit down and discuss what they were doing with this whole... thing. But to do that, she would need clothes. No way could she have a rational discussion about relationships in the nude. She needed armor for something so potentially vulnerability-inducing.

She started to rise from the bed, moving to lift Lincoln's arm from where it lay, draped atop her, cuddling her close. Who knew the guy was a cuddler? But before she could move, he shifted.

"Mm, morning." His husky, sleep-roughened voice filled her ear as he tightened his arm around her, kissing her softly on the neck. "Planning on running out on me again?"

A tiny fleck of guilt hampered her pleasant morning mood. Did he have to keep bringing up her do-and-dash moment?

"No." She shifted on the bed, turning over on her side to face him. "I was simply going to get up and head to the kitchen to see if there was any coffee I could make."

He grinned, full lips peeking out from his close-cropped dark beard, which, yes, she found insanely attractive.

"Liar."

Maybe, but she wasn't ready to admit her morning-after jitters. Not without clothes, anyway.

"Regardless, we should be heading out soon. The cleaning company will be here at noon, and the house needs to be empty so they can do their job."

Lincoln yawned, arms stretching over his head as his jaw cracked. "I suppose you're right."

He kissed her cheek before pushing up from the bed, naked and completely at ease with his nudity. Hey, she wasn't complaining. Not when she got to lie there and reap the benefits. The room had chilled slightly over the long night, but Lilly suddenly felt very hot as she stared at the fine, round firmness of Lincoln's backside. The man had an ass you could bounce a quarter off of. She remembered he said something once about being a runner. It fit with his lean physique. He wasn't overly muscular, but his body was honed. Tight. Scrumptious.

"Uh, Lilly?"

At his worried tone, she reluctantly drew her focus off his runner buns and glanced at his face. He stood at the window, curtains slightly parted, his face swiveling from her to the view outside and back.

"Yes?"

He winced, sucking air in through his teeth. "I don't think we're getting out of here today."

"What? Why?"

Grabbing the comforter from the bed, she wrapped it around her as she stood. Not because she was ashamed of her nudity, but because the room was slightly chilly. She might not be a supermodel, but she knew she looked pretty good naked. Lincoln had nothing but praise to say about her unclothed form—or any of her forms, for that matter.

Slipping her glasses on, she headed over to his side. A gasp escaped her lips as she fingered the curtain and peeled it back. The sight that hit her was beautiful and dreadful all at the same time. "Oh no!"

"I don't think the cleaning company will be making it up today, either."

She glared at Lincoln, but the smart-ass simply smiled back. With a sigh, she glanced out the window again to see the fluffy, swirling white snowflakes fall from the sky to join the three feet of snow already on the ground. How bad had the storm gotten last night after everyone left? Must have been a doozy to leave this much fresh powder in just a few hours.

"I hope everyone got home okay." She turned to grab her phone from the pocket of her dress, which Lincoln had tossed on the floor at the foot of the bed last night before blowing her freaking mind. "I need to check in with Mo."

Her friend wasn't the best at driving in the snow, and she'd left the latest. But Lilly's worry wasn't necessary. As she retrieved her cell phone, she saw she had two texts from her roommate time-stamped late last night. The first read, *Just got home. The roads are getting bad. You two better stay put.* She breathed out a sigh of relief knowing her friend was safe in their apartment. The second text made her laugh as she read, *And you better have lots of hot, wild sex and tell me all about it when you get home!*

The first, they'd already done; the second, she would in no way do. She loved Mo, but there were some things you didn't share, even with your closest friends.

"Mo okay?" Lincoln asked from his spot at the window.

She nodded. "Yup. She got home safe and sound." Which meant everyone else most likely had, too.

"What do we do now?"

She stared at him, her gaze shifting to the beautiful yet inconvenient storm outside. "Well, I need to call the cleaning service and reschedule for tomorrow. And I should also call the property manager and explain the situation. Hopefully they won't charge us for an extra day, but if they do, I'll make sure Marie and Kenneth won't be charged for it."

Her clients had already left. They couldn't control the weather. No way would she let them be charged an additional fee. Lilly was positive the property manager wouldn't charge them an extra day due to weather conditions. Most Colorado businesses were used to dealing with snow snafus like this.

"Wasn't worried for a second." Lincoln grinned. "Besides, I'm sure you can work your superhero magic and get them to agree to an extra day rental at no charge."

If he kept being so wonderful, she would have no choice but to fall for him.

Liar. Like you haven't fallen for him already.

She cleared her throat, shaking the thought from her head. "Let's just take this one step at a time."

She lifted her phone to call the cleaners. Lincoln crossed the room, kissing her cheek and whispering a "good luck" before he made his way to the attached bathroom. He left the door open a crack, and within seconds she heard the shower turn on. Hopefully these calls went quickly, because she really wanted to join him in that shower. To conserve water. They were in the midst of a storm, after all. Had to conserve energy and so on.

The call to the cleaning company was quick, as the staff had not left the city yet and happily agreed to come out tomorrow instead. The call to the property manager took a bit longer, as she had to contact the mayor's office due to the storm and no one was in the office. It took a bit of searching to find the mayor's home number, but when she did, he quickly agreed with her decision to have the house cleaned tomorrow instead of today.

Lincoln might have something on his superhero theory, because the mayor didn't charge her another day but thanked her for staying and keeping an eye on the place, even going so far as to offer her a discount the next time she booked an event.

With responsibilities crossed off her mental list, she dropped the blanket and headed toward the bathroom, pausing to snag a condom from the nightstand on her way. A wall of hot steam hit her face as she pushed open the bathroom door. The space was as luxurious as the rest of the room. A double vanity sat against the back wall, and black-framed mirrors hung over a marble countertop. The toilet was off to the side in a small room with a door that closed off to the rest of the bathroom.

"Lilly? Is that you?"

She craned her neck, squinting through the mist as it fogged up her glasses.

"Yes, it's me."

"Everything work out okay?"

She stared, trying to make out his form behind the glass of the large shower, but everything was distorted and hazy.

"Yes, everything is set for tomorrow, and there's no extra charge for acts of extreme weather."

His chuckle rose over the pounding sound of the water. "Great, then you can come in here and let me wash…your back."

A giddy thrill shot through her at the notion of all Lincoln could *wash* for her. But first, Mother Nature called.

"Give me one second."

She headed into the tiny toilet room and took care of business. The condom packet still in hand, she then made her way to the large shower, leaving her glasses on the sink countertop. Slowly, she pulled open the glass door and stepped inside. Lincoln's blurry face came into focus as he wrapped an arm around her waist, pulling her into him.

"Hi," he said, kissing her lips softly.

"Hi," she returned the greeting and the kiss.

"Is that a condom packet in your hand or are you just happy to see me?"

She snorted, water spraying her in the face when Lincoln tilted his head in question.

"It's a condom," she confirmed. "And you have the absolute worst sex humor."

"I didn't know it was a competition." He grinned, turning them so the showerhead hit her back.

Warm, pounding water massaged her shoulders as Lincoln's hands caressed her lower back.

"You know," he said between rubs. "Shower sex isn't as hot as the movies make it out to be."

"I know." She moaned as his hands dipped lower, grasping the globes of her ass and kneading in a sensual manner. "But I figured we could give it a shot. See if we can make some Hollywood magic."

He chuckled, lips brushing against hers as one finger dipped in between her thighs to stroke her right where she ached for him.

"For you, sweetheart, I'm willing to give anything a shot."

She tried not to read too much into that statement. This was just sex talk. They were in the throes of passion. Promises made here weren't to be taken seriously. That's how her mom got her heart broken so often—she believed what men said when they were naked. You could never believe what a man said when he was naked…or what a woman said when she was naked, either. The loss of clothes directly correlated to the loss of pragmatic brain cells.

All thoughts left her mind the moment Lincoln plunged two fingers inside her. Her body tightened with need.

"Lincoln," she gasped, warm water from the showerhead trickling into her mouth as her head tilted up.

"I've got you, sweetheart. Tell me what you want."

"You." She reached out, grasping the hard length of his erection pressing against her belly and stroking. "I want you. Inside me. Now."

He laughed softly. "One of us is going to have to stop playing so we can put the condom on."

But she didn't want to stop playing, and she didn't want him to stop, either. Why weren't humans made with three arms? Just think of all the life problems that could be solved by an extra appendage.

"Lilly," he pressed as she quickened her strokes. "I don't want to stop touching you."

Good. She didn't want him to stop, and she also didn't want to stop. On the other hand, she wanted more of him inside her. A, ahem, bigger part of him inside her.

"Hold out the condom," he demanded.

Their occupied hands still working magic on each other, Lilly held up the foil packet. Lincoln maneuvered them again so the water hit his back, blocking the stream from their good bits. He grasped the corner of the foil and ripped, gripping the latex protection between his fingers and pulling it from the wrapper.

That was a new one for her. She'd never shared opening a condom with a partner before. It felt intimate in a way far deeper than it should be. Not wanting to deal with that emotion right now, she dropped the wrapper and gently plucked the condom from his fingers and rolled it on his length, replacing her other hand but continuing to stroke him as she rolled the latex down his cock.

"Now, Lilly," he growled, grasping her thigh and pulling her leg over his hip.

"Now," she agreed.

His fingers left her only to be replaced a moment later by the blunt head of his erection. She gasped as he pushed in those first few inches.

"Fuck me!" he groaned.

She smiled. "Happy to."

He grinned a moment before his mouth descended on hers. As he kissed the living daylights out of her, he backed them against the shower wall, thrusting inside her in a slow, easy rhythm. The stall was so big, the water no longer hit them, but the steam rose around them, heating the already scorching air as they moved with a single-minded focus. His tongue played with hers, tasting, worshipping, devouring her every breath. Her mind fell completely blank, the only thoughts filling it Lincoln and the way he made her feel.

She felt the crescendo coming, her thigh tightening around his hip. He instinctively knew what she wanted, quickening his pace, pounding into her until her body exploded with a rapturous delight of gratification. Lincoln surged against her twice more, elongating her delicious ride on cloud nine. She felt him pulse as he found his own release.

"Okay," he panted, pulling his lips from hers. "Now that proved the Hollywood theory right, I'd say."

She'd agree, but she didn't have any air left in her lungs to form words, so she just nodded.

"Come on." He kissed her temple. "Let's wash up and then see if there's any food left in this place."

Once they finished rinsing off, Lilly headed upstairs to grab her bags and bring them down to Lincoln's room. No sense in keeping them upstairs, since she planned to spend every second with the man for the next day. Preferably naked.

After they dressed—boo—they headed to the kitchen, where they found the catering staff had left plenty of extra food and wedding cake for the cleaning staff. Lilly made a mental note to give the cleaning company extra cash to make up for what she and Lincoln would consume.

They cobbled together a breakfast of rolls and fruit, choosing to leave the heavy dinner food and cake for later. Luckily, the rental came equipped with a pantry filled with nonperishable items, including the most important of substances: coffee.

They enjoyed their makeshift breakfast, debating whether or not to go outside and enjoy the snowfall, but since neither of them had any protective snow clothes, they opted to stay inside and enjoy the weather from the large windows. Lincoln found a chessboard, and they played a few games.

"Well, it's official," Lincoln said with a frown. "We are as bad at chess as we are good at pinball."

Lilly laughed, but she had to agree. "It might help if we knew the rules a little bit better."

"Hey, you never did tell me how you became so good at pinball."

She shifted in the large leather chair, grabbing one of the pawns she'd captured from Lincoln and rubbing the cool marble piece between her fingers as she spoke. "My mom's second husband was a huge gamer guy. Video games, board games—you name it, he played it."

His eyes lit up. "*D&D?*"

"Yes, you nerd." She laughed. "Even *D&D*."

Placing the tiny game piece back on the table, she removed her glasses to clean them with the edge of her shirt even though there wasn't a smudge on them.

"Anyway, he was a good guy. One of the few I really liked. I was twelve when they got together, so peak awkward preteen stage. Curt—that was his name—he tried to teach me every game he owned, but the only one I really liked was pinball."

She sighed, a small smile curling her lips at the memory. "He had this great machine in the garage. It was a zombie-themed one. Classic. I spent hours playing that thing and even beat his high score."

"Did that upset him?" Lincoln asked, his voice filled with concern.

She shook her head with a smile. "Quite the opposite. He took me out for ice cream and declared me the pinball champion."

"Sounds like a great guy."

He was. It absolutely crushed her when Curt and her mother divorced. More than any other failed relationship her mom had. And Curt… He'd been so devastated, but he told Lilly he and her mother were just too different to be together. The spark had died, and they didn't have enough in common to keep them together.

They didn't match.

She shook off the melancholy memory. "Anyway, after he and my mom split, we moved out. I started playing pinball at the local arcade whenever the stress of…life got to be too much." She let out a wistful sigh. "Never found another zombie pinball machine as cool as Curt's, though. I miss that game."

The glasses she clutched in her hands were suddenly pulled away. She glanced up as a blurry Lincoln crouched down in front of her. When had he moved from his seat across the table? He slid her glasses back onto her face with so much gentle care her throat tightened.

"I'm sure he missed you, too, Lilly. Anyone would."

The soft conviction of his statement made her heart swell and crack at the same time. She'd never told anyone about Curt and the pinball machine before. Her friends just thought she learned in middle school at the arcade. How had this man gotten past her defenses? Why did she feel safe sharing these parts of herself she'd never shown anyone else?

"Hungry?"

She latched on to his simple question, choosing to shove her more complicated ones deep down in her brain to pull out later and examine.

Much, much later.

"Yeah." She placed a soft kiss to his lips. "Let's go see what we can throw together."

After more leftovers for lunch, they headed to the entertainment room on the third floor, which housed a large TV and an extensive DVD collection. She picked a comedy Lincoln said he'd always wanted to see, and they snuggled on the couch as the movie played. After scrounging up some food for dinner, they headed back to the bedroom, where he spent half the night worshipping her body over and over again.

Honestly, it was the most fun Lilly had ever had being snowed in, and that scared her. Because she wasn't afraid she *might* be falling for Lincoln.

She had fallen. And hard.

Chapter Seventeen

Lincoln woke up for the second morning in a row with a soft, warm Lilly Walsh wrapped in his arms. He had to say, it was a pretty fantastic way to wake up. The way they'd gone to bed last night had been even better. Spending the entire day with her yesterday—no wedding business, no plans, just casual, hanging-out fun—had been a blast. He couldn't remember a day he'd so thoroughly enjoyed. It was great.

And now it was over.

They'd left the curtains open last night to watch the snowfall, since no one was around for miles. The soft swirl of the flakes falling from the sky had lulled his already-spent body to sleep. Lilly mentioned it felt like they were traveling through space and the snowflakes were stars. The only stars he saw were the ones in her beautiful green eyes.

Corny? Maybe, but the woman made him feel corny, and needy, and happy, and other emotions he wasn't sure what to do with at the moment.

But now sunlight poured in through the clear glass frames of the window. The storm had stopped at some point over the night. The roads might still be a bit hazardous, but he assumed the plows had been out by now to clear off the highway. Since most of their driving would be interstate bound, he supposed that meant they had to get a move on. Damn. He didn't want to leave. He didn't want to move right now. Lying in bed with Lilly in his arms was damn near perfection.

"Is it morning already?" the woman on his mind asked with a yawn.

He tightened his arm around her, squeezing slightly while kissing her temple softly. "Unfortunately, yes. And the snow has stopped."

She turned to face him, a slight frown on her face. "I guess that means we should pack up and get out of here. The cleaners said they'd be here around noon."

As much as he knew she was right, a part of him didn't want to leave this magical little sanctuary they'd created, a place where the outside world, their differences and difficulties, couldn't intrude. At least he didn't have to worry about her *no dating clients* rule anymore. Marie and Kenneth were now a happily married couple and no longer in business with Mile High Happiness, which made him free to pursue dating Lilly. If she wanted that, too. Based on her enthusiastic participation over the past twenty-four hours, he hoped she did.

"It's only..." He leaned to the nightstand to check his phone. "Eight fifteen. We have a few hours before they arrive."

Her eyebrows bobbed up and down. "Whatever will we do?"

He had some ideas. Judging from the small, soft, wandering hand currently working its way to his morning wood, she had the same idea he did. Grabbing a condom from the box on the nightstand—which they'd worked through quite thoroughly since the night of the wedding—Lilly moved to straddle him. He let out a fierce groan as she took him in her hand, stroking his hardness in a slow, agonizingly erotic fashion.

"Sweetheart." He reached for her, but she pushed his hands above his head.

"No. No touching." She gave him a wicked grin. "My turn to play."

He loved it when she got all bossy. Ten minutes later, he was ready to cry uncle, but since he wasn't inside Lilly yet, he did his damnedest to hold off.

"Lilly! I need you."

Was he begging? Who the hell cared if he was? He'd crawl on his hands and knees through a pile of broken glass just to be with this woman. Okay, maybe that was a bit overdramatic, but if he was going to keep from embarrassing himself and disappointing her, he needed to be inside her.

Now.

The sexy little minx laughed, ripping open the condom and rolling it down his swollen length. She lifted herself, slowly, excruciatingly slowly, lowering herself onto him. Though he'd like to claim he rocked her world, with Lilly on top, the show was hers. And what a show. In less than five minutes, she had them both crying out with the force of their combined orgasms as she collapsed on his chest.

Huh, he didn't know that was even possible. Lincoln always made sure his lovers were satisfied, but he'd never experienced reaching completion at the same time before.

It felt special, significant.

"Wow." He breathed out the word on the last bit of air left in his lungs.

She laughed softly. "You can say that again."

"Wow," he repeated with a grin.

She lightly smacked him on the shoulder. "Smart-ass."

A small ache tugged in his chest, something that

suspiciously resembled feelings. He pushed it down. He and Lilly were casual. Fun. He didn't want anything deeper, so he refused to acknowledge the weird sensation in his gut. But not wanting to get too serious with her didn't mean he didn't want to know more about the fascinating woman in his arms.

He pulled her in close to his side, absently playing with the dark, silky strands of her hair as he spoke. "Since I'm no longer part of it, wanna tell me about this mysterious rule you have against relationships with members of your wedding party?"

She stiffened slightly. "How do you know it's my rule?"

"Lilly." She was deflecting. He didn't know why it was so important to him to know the reason. He should be happy with the sex and leave it at that. Why was he so adamant about getting to know her better? He wanted fun, not a serious relationship. Right?

His brain was a jumbled mess at the moment. Eh, maybe he should blame it on all the amazing sex. Or maybe he was using that as a cover for something he didn't want to admit to.

That maybe Lilly was coming to mean more to him than he ever planned.

"Fine, you annoyingly persistent man. I'll tell you. But it's not a happy story."

He didn't like the way her voice quieted with that, the soft, almost shame-filled tone taking over. Holding her tight, he kissed the top of her head.

"You can tell me." He meant that, too. She could tell him anything. Despite all their differences, he felt this weird connection to Lilly. As if they were two odd shapes that fit together perfectly, complementing each other in a way no one else could. He shut that thought down right away. That sounded far too much like deep feelings. Something he promised himself he wouldn't do again.

"Okay, here goes." She cleared her throat, voice taking

on that confident, in-charge tone he heard her use when solving problems. "About five years ago, when our business was pretty new, we were planning this wedding for a very nice couple. They had a large budget and a lot of requests. I was in constant contact with them and members of their party. Over the first few months, I got to know their best man fairly well."

A wave of jealousy washed over him. Ridiculous. Lilly was a grown woman. Of course she'd had other relationships before him. Hell, he'd been married before. It would be ludicrous to think the woman hadn't been involved with another man. Didn't stop the caveman instinct in his gut from wanting to pound the other guy into oblivion. Or at least hack his computer and fill it with viruses.

"You started seeing each other?"

He felt her soft hair brush against his jaw as she nodded, a few strands getting caught in his beard.

"Yes, he was charming and good-looking, and I guess I got swept up in it all a little. But he wanted to keep the relationship a secret."

Red flag! Secret relationships were never a good thing. He'd seen enough romantic dramas to know that. And yes, he was a man who loved romantic movies, despite how much his fellow software engineers liked to razz him about it. They could all go screw themselves. A good movie was a good movie.

"Like a dope, I agreed. And then..."

Oh shit. He didn't like the sound of where this story was going. Did the jackass break her heart?

"Did he hurt you?" he asked, trying to mask the whirling rage of emotions inside.

She shook her head. "Not in any physical sense of the word."

When she didn't elaborate, he pressed, "What happened?"

A weary sigh left her. "His wife showed up."

Lincoln tensed, his entire body freezing at her words. *His wife.* The guy had been married. A cheater. Lincoln knew firsthand how that could rip a person's world apart. Tear down your entire belief system with one fell swoop. Change who you thought you were and had been as a person.

All the positive and slightly scary feelings of the past twenty-four hours flew away, his body turning to ice as her confession pounded over and over in his head.

Lilly had slept with a married man.

She probably hadn't known. The Lilly he knew wouldn't intentionally hurt someone like that. *I thought Jessa wouldn't hurt me, either.* The dark cloud of his past experiences created a haze of anger over any logic. How well did he know Lilly, really? He'd known his ex for years, and she still betrayed him, so why did he think he'd know a woman he'd only talked with for a few weeks and slept with a few times any better?

He stood, unable to sit next to her as she continued her story, his mind refusing to separate what happened to him and what Lilly was telling him. It all swirled together in a confusing, jumbled mess.

"He told me he wanted to keep our relationship a secret because he didn't want to take away from his friend's special day. Turns out his wife, the bride's cousin, was serving overseas and got some kind of special pass to come surprise everyone for the week of the wedding. I had no idea he was married. If I had, I never would have looked twice at the scumbag."

So she hadn't known he was married. Of course she hadn't. That information should make him feel better, but somehow, it didn't. Lilly hadn't intentionally harmed another's marriage, so why couldn't he look at her? Why did the sickness in his gut start spreading out into his entire body, filling him with nothing but anger and betrayal?

"When our clients found out, they sued us. The bride was

furious at what I'd done. I was disgusted with myself for my part, even though I had no idea the asshole was married. We almost lost the business."

Which would explain her rule.

"I'm not a cheater, Lincoln." The soft but fierce declaration was whispered at his continued silence.

He knew how hard it must have been for her to share such a personal and painful bit of her past. Logically, he even knew she hadn't been at fault for what happened. But he just couldn't get over the fact that Lilly had slept with a married man. He felt the betrayal from his wife's infidelity all over again. This had nothing to do with him, he knew that, but his rational brain wasn't in charge at the moment.

Right now, all he could do was feel. And all he was feeling was pain.

He was just letting his past color the situation. As much as he'd wish it otherwise, her revelation had shocked him back to that angry, bitter husband who'd discovered the woman he once loved, the woman he'd promised to be faithful and true to, had not honored her vow to do the same. It wasn't fair to either of them, but here they were.

"Lincoln?"

He turned at the hesitant call of his name to see Lilly sitting in the bed, blanket pulled up to her chin like a shield. He saw the question in her eyes, the need for him to reassure her that everything was okay, that this didn't change anything.

But it did. He couldn't help his past, and neither could she.

"I'm sorry, I'm just... I'm going to take a shower." He turned to head into the bathroom, unable to face the pain and disappointment in her eyes. "You should probably pack your things. We wanna get out of here before the cleaners come, right?"

He strode toward the bathroom with a single-minded

purpose, pushing down all the messy, confusing feelings inside and shutting the door behind him. He cranked the water up as hot as it would go, letting the pounding jets redden his skin, wishing they could burn away all this ugly pain inside, all the while his mind filling with the image of the anguish on Lilly's face as he'd dismissed her.

He'd screwed up. And he didn't know how to fix it or even if he wanted to.

You jackass, of course you do. Lilly is amazing, and you're being a dick.

True. But he didn't know how to get over the spike of agony he'd felt the moment she revealed the man she'd slept with had been married. *She didn't know!* He had to remind himself of that. It wasn't Lilly's fault. The logical side of him wanted to find the asshole and pummel him. Not only for hurting Lilly and dragging her into the whole sordid thing, but also for hurting his wife by cheating. Both women had been wronged, and the only person to blame was the man who'd lied.

The water started to go cold, and he turned off the tap, now feeling doubly like a dick for taking all the hot water. But when he came out of the bathroom five minutes later, Lilly was fully dressed in a pair of black slacks and a crisp white button-down shirt. Her hair had been twisted into a bun on the top of her head. Glasses covering her eyes but in no way shielding the stony expression in her gaze.

"I'll only be a minute," he said, grabbing his bag of clothes and heading back into the bathroom.

Lilly took a giant step backward as he approached. He didn't miss the significance of the move. The woman didn't want him within touching distance. He couldn't say he blamed her. He was being an ass.

"Be quick, please." She lifted her chin, tossing back her shoulders. "I'm going to make a final check of the house, and

I need to lock up after all parties leave the premises."

All parties, she'd said. Not *them*. He'd gone back to being a client relation. How the hell could he have screwed this all up so badly? He needed to talk to her, to explain where his knee-jerk reaction had come from. But doing that would open up a wound he wasn't sure he was ready to reveal to her.

Still, she deserved some kind of explanation.

"Lilly, I—"

"Make sure you don't leave anything you value behind or it will be thrown out."

With those parting words, she turned and headed out of the room. Lincoln made his way into the bathroom and quickly dressed. He packed up all his stuff, checking the room once more to make sure they left nothing behind.

The bed was rumpled, sheets askew. He grabbed the comforter from the floor where Lilly left it and tossed it on top of the bed. It hung off the edge at his lackluster throw, then slowly slipped to the floor. The perfect metaphor for how this morning had gone. From sex-strewn sheets to a huge, suffocating blanket slowly sliding, all the pleasant memories crashing to the floor.

He left the room and headed for the front door, where an impatient Lilly waited, foot tapping in her black pumps.

"I hope you have a scraper in your car, because the storm covered it in snow."

Lilly had driven up with Mo for the wedding, and since the woman left the night of, that meant Lincoln would be driving her home. A fact that had excited him just a few hours ago but now sounded like the worst drive of his life. He knew by the set of her shoulders that she didn't want to hear any explanation for his behavior this morning. He wasn't even sure he could give her one right now. Her reveal was too fresh in his mind.

It was going to be a long, silent, tense drive back to the

city.

"I do." He grabbed his keys from his jacket pocket. "It's in my trunk. Wait here while I take care of it."

She nodded, eyes focused on the snow outside. He made his way into the chilly February-morning air. The sun shone brightly, a mocking juxtaposition to his current mood. He opened the driver-side door to insert the key and start the car, blasting the heat and defrosters so the vehicle would be warm once he finished scraping.

After tossing his bag in the trunk and grabbing the snow scraper, he went to work brushing the fluffy snow off the car's windows, roof, and hood. It took a few more minutes for him to scrape the ice that had frozen overnight. Once he finished and the car was ready to hit the road, he replaced the scraper in the trunk, turning to get Lilly. But the woman already stood outside, locking the cabin door. She strode toward him as if she were walking a red carpet instead of trudging through a few feet of snow. He noticed she prudently placed each of her steps in the footfalls he'd made.

"Hop in. I've got the heater going. It should be warm."

She said nothing, moving to the front passenger side and sliding in. She buckled up and placed her bag on her lap, grip tight as she leaned to the side, as far away from the driver's side as possible.

Yup. This was going to be a really long drive.

Chapter Eighteen

Men are stupid.

Lilly had no idea why her confession turned Lincoln from fiery lover to ice man. He hadn't once tried to contact her since he dropped her off at her building two days ago. Not that she'd tried to contact him, either, but he had been the one who said they should go on a date, the one who pursued her this whole time, the one who bought her a drink in the bar all those weeks ago. Why was he suddenly Mr. Silent now?

Because you slept with him. Didn't you learn anything from your mother?

No. She would not listen to that nasty little voice in her head. Lincoln wasn't like all the men her mother dated. He wasn't the type of guy to get his jollies from a woman, then ghost her. He'd already had her once. If he didn't want something real, a true relationship, he wouldn't have kept trying to start something up again.

Right?

Maybe she was just as delusional as her mother when it came to men.

"Okay, spill."

At Mo's demand, Lilly glanced up from the open file she'd been staring at but in no way reading.

"Huh? Spill what?"

The smaller woman rose from her desk, making her way across the office to pop her hip on the edge of Lilly's.

"The reason you've been all mopey the past two days."

She scowled at her roommate's assumption. "I have not been mopey."

"I'm sorry, sweetie," Pru said, rising to join Mo. "But you kind of have been a bit of a grumpapotamus."

Mo arched an eyebrow. "Grumpapotamus?"

Pru winced. "I'm really trying to clean up my potty mouth before the twins start talking. Finn swears Simon said 'dada' the other day, but I think he was just burping. We're trying to cut out the naughty stuff so we don't have toddlers shouting the f-word in the aisle of a crowded restaurant."

Lilly smiled. The first genuine one she'd felt in days. See, who needed a stupid man when she had her friends?

Mo chuckled. "I think I was that toddler."

"Big surprise," Pru deadpanned.

The image of toddler Mo sitting in a restaurant, swinging her legs while innocently shouting obscenities, made Lilly lose it. She tipped back her head, boisterous laughter escaping her lips. She slapped a hand over her mouth, but that just made her snort out her nose, which in turn led to more laughter. Mo quickly joined in the hilarity. Lilly had no idea if her roommate was laughing with her or at her, but it didn't matter. It felt good to laugh again. The past few days, she'd felt like a dark storm cloud hung over her head. Raining on every thought she had. Dampening her mood, no matter how hard she tried to smile.

"I wish my parents found it as funny as you, Lilly." Mo smiled. "They took away my favorite crayons for two days when I said 'shit' during dinner with Nonna. On the bright side, it got you to smile for the first time since you came storming into the apartment the other morning."

Lilly sighed. Mo could be a bit overdramatic. "I did not storm."

"You most certainly did." Her roommate pointed a finger in her face. "You stormed to your room while muttering something about stupid men and slammed the door behind you before I could even get in a hello."

Affronted at the accusation, she gasped. "I didn't slam the door!"

"Fine. You shut it very firmly. But it was obvious you were—and still are—upset. Spill. Did things not go well with Lincoln? Was the sex not as good as you remembered? Did he ask for weird stuff?"

"Oh please, Mo." Pru chuckled. "Like you wouldn't do weird stuff."

"*I* would, but Lilly wouldn't."

Hey, she'd do weird stuff! Maybe. Depending on what it was and who asked. To be honest, she'd be open to a hell of a lot with Lincoln. She trusted the man. Or she had. Before she shared the worst moment of her life with him and he acted like she was the one to blame.

She glanced at the two women before her. Her business partners, her friends. These women who had stood by her side through thick and thin for more than a decade. They were closer than friends. They were sisters. They were family. A family of their choosing, and that made them bonded in a way unlike any other.

She knew they would always be there for her and vice versa. It hadn't been fair of her to shut them out the past few days. She should have discussed things with them right away, but a small part of her felt ashamed. Worried she'd fallen into the trap of her mother.

Her friends weren't here to judge her. They didn't do that. They helped one another. The time had come for her to accept their help and start sharing. If nothing else, talking about it out loud might help her solve the hot-and-cold mystery that was Lincoln Reid.

"He didn't ask for any weird stuff," she started. "And, no, the sex wasn't as good as I remembered." Mo's lips turned down into a little frown until Lilly added, "It was better."

"Hot damn! I knew just by looking at him that man could set fire to a bed."

He could indeed. He could also pour a giant bucket of ice-cold water all over it. Metaphorically speaking, of course.

"If things were so great, why the storm clouds?" Pru reached out to place a sympathetic hand over Lilly's.

Of course, her friends would be able to tell she was under a gloom cloud. When you lived with someone for a decade—as they had done—you got to know a person really well. There was no sense in hiding anything from them.

"Everything was going great." She lifted her shoulders, shaking her head as she recounted the weekend. "The wedding went off without a hitch. After everyone left, I went to Lincoln's room to...um, you know."

"Screw his brains out?"

"Classy, Mo." Pru shook her head, motioning for Lilly to continue.

"Anyway, we had...an amazing night." There was no other way to describe it without setting off the sprinklers. "Then, when we woke up, the storm had really rolled in."

Pru gasped. "Did you get stuck up there?"

She nodded. Mo knew that from her text saying she wouldn't be home, but Pru didn't live with them anymore, since she got together with Finn. As happy as she was for her friend starting a family and getting married, a part of her grieved the loss of the tight-knit sisterhood the three of them once shared. But that was the way of life. Things changed, people moved on, relationships shifted.

"Oh, I get it now!" Mo exclaimed. "You all got stuck up there, but Lincoln only brought one condom and you couldn't get your freak on anymore. Men are idiots. So unprepared. That's why I always carry a box of condoms in my purse. Never rely on your partner for protection."

"No." Lilly bit her lip, cheeks flaming as memories of just how prepared Lincoln had been filled her mind. "We were very much covered in that department."

"Oh really?" Mo bobbed her eyebrows. "Care to elaborate?"

"Ignore her." Pru lifted a hand to block out their brazen friend. "Continue with your story."

Skipping the more intimate details, she launched into the activities they'd done to keep themselves busy during the storm. How comfortable they'd been chatting, scrounging for food, playing games, watching movies. It amazed her how normal it had all felt. Like they'd been doing it for years. Hanging out with Lincoln, even when they weren't having sex, felt good. Right. Like home.

Mo scrunched up her nose when Lilly finished. "Okay, soooo what happened? Why the Debbie Downer routine?"

"I told him." She swallowed past the painful lump of emotion clogging her throat. "About what happened. The worst man we do not speak of."

"That bastard," Mo spat. "I still wish you would have let me kick him in the balls for what he did to you and his wife."

She gave a watery laugh. "I'm over it, Mo. Really."

And the odd thing was, she was telling the truth. For years, she'd blamed herself, thinking she should have seen the signs, but the truth was she'd believed a person she had no reason to doubt. That wasn't being naive; it was just being human. She might always feel bad about what happened, but over the years, and with the constant support of her friends, Lilly now knew what happened wasn't her fault. She'd simply chosen to trust the wrong person.

Happened to a lot of people.

"But when I told Lincoln, he...tensed."

Pru tilted her head. "Tensed?"

"Yeah, and he... I can't be certain because he didn't really say anything, but I got the feeling he..."

"He what, sweetie?" Pru asked.

She glanced at her friends, her heart cracking as she spoke the words out loud. "I get the feeling he blames me for what happened."

"That bastard!" Mo swore again. "Let me make him some of my special brownies, Lilly, please."

Since she knew her roommate's *special* brownies were not the kind sold in the dispensaries around Colorado but instead could be used for backed-up seniors at the retirement homes, she shook her head with a smile. She wouldn't stoop to such an immature level. No matter how much she secretly wanted to.

"Thanks for the offer, Mo, but no. My first assessment was right." Taking a fortifying breath, she lifted her chin. "Lincoln and I aren't a good match."

"So what?" Pru said. "Take a look at the three of us. Look how different we are. Would anyone ever think we'd be best friends?"

Pru had a point. She loved her best friends fiercely, but their personalities and interests were in direct opposition a lot of the time. "Friends and romantic relationships are different."

"Says who?" Mo argued. "Both bring joy into your lives. Both are there to support you, encourage you, share ups and downs with you. The only difference with Lincoln is he satisfies your carnal needs as well as your emotional ones.

Who cares if you don't have every single thing in common?"

She wanted to believe that. So very badly, but... "We had some fun, but now it's over. Time to move on. Better now than before any serious feelings started to develop."

"Oh please," Mo snorted. "That ship has already sailed, Lil."

"What are you talking about?"

"You guys spark."

"We what?"

"Spark." Mo smiled, her eyes filling with excitement. "Any time you were in the room together. No, actually, any time you even thought about each other, everyone could see it on your faces."

She scoffed but couldn't stop from asking, "See what?"

"The spark of utter and complete happiness you ignited in each other."

What a load of nonsense. "It's called lust, Mo. It's not real. A temporary chemical reaction people share when sexually attracted to each other. It fades and dies, usually not at the same rate for both parties, and someone ends up getting hurt. Just ask my mother."

"Oh, sweetie." Pru shook her head. "You know we would never say anything bad about your mom, but she's not a good person to judge relationships on. She doesn't have a spark with every man she dates. She has an inability to differentiate lust from love."

Lilly bit her lip, clearing her throat as it clogged with fear and blinking back the tears threatening to spill from her eyes. "And what if I have the same problem?"

Mo laughed, not harshly but with soft love. "Lil, in all the years I've known you, I've never seen you lose your head over a guy like you have with Lincoln."

"You always keep people at a safe distance. Even us, sometimes," Pru chimed in. "And that's okay," she rushed to add as Lilly started to protest. "We know it's hard for you to open up emotionally. We all have baggage from our past to deal with, but we love you and you love us."

She nodded, a few tears slipping free.

"And as much as I was resistant to it before," Pru said with a small smile, "I think you might care, deeply, for Lincoln?"

Again, she nodded. But she feared what her friends were leaving unsaid was true. She didn't just care for Lincoln. She loved him. And that's why his dismissal hurt and confused her so much.

Dang it! She had told her heart to stay out of this, and the damn thing refused. This was supposed to be a fun thing, not a falling-in-love thing.

Then why am I so sad it's over?

No. Not sad. She was devastated. More than any other loss she'd felt.

Exactly when and where had she fallen in love with Lincoln? Ugh, she'd like to go back to that moment and smack some sense into herself.

Too late now. Apparently, according to her friends and her heart, she was in love with a nerdy computer geek who told bad pirate jokes that made her laugh, kicked her butt at pinball, and made her feel more than any man she'd ever known. Maybe her friends were right. Life didn't always set you up with who you thought you should fit with. So what if they didn't match in every area of life? Not everyone had to be perfectly compatible.

She wasn't even sure that was a possibility anymore. All she knew was that without Lincoln in her life, something felt...wrong. A part of her was missing, and she didn't think she'd be whole again if she didn't get it back.

Would she ever be able to tell him how she truly felt?

"I'm sorry if I ever pushed you two away." She spoke through her tears, not wanting to miss an opportunity to tell the people she cared about exactly how she felt. "I know it's sometimes hard for me to show it, but I do love you both. And I'm really happy I have you in my life."

"Awwww." Mo pressed her hands to her chest, rushing around the desk, opening her arms wide. "Come here, you."

"Group hug!" Pru squeezed her from one side while Mo attacked her on the other. "We love you, too, sweetie."

She endured the hug for fifteen seconds—emotional vulnerability was one thing, but she really liked her personal space—before gently rolling her chair back and breaking out of the embrace.

"What do you think I should do?"

Her friends shared a look, silently communicating before turning back to her.

"Call him," Pru said.

"Yes," Mo agreed. "Ask him to go for drinks to talk. Hash it all out."

"Communication is the key to a healthy relationship. Believe me."

Since Pru was currently happily married to the love of her life, Lilly would trust her on this. Gathering up all her courage, she grabbed her cell phone and sent off a text, for once acting with her heart instead of her brain.

Chapter Nineteen

What the hell am I doing here?

The thought popped into Lincoln's head for the third time since he'd stepped foot into 1up. The same answer kept coming back to him. He was here because Lilly texted asking to grab a drink and talk. She deserved an explanation for his shitty behavior the other morning and his avoidance the past few days. He wasn't exactly sure what he was going to say to explain things.

How about the truth, dumbass?

He sighed, taking a sip of the stout in front of him. The rich almost-coffee-like flavor of the local brew did nothing to improve his mood. Usually a good stout could cure all his ails, but not tonight. Because he knew that in order to truly apologize to Lilly, he would have to explain. And explaining meant opening up. Something he was not good at since his ex ripped his world out from under him.

This was going to suck. But Lilly deserved the truth. She deserved a hell of a lot more, too. The woman was amazing, so tough and in charge while at the same time caring and soft.

She deserved better than a man who didn't even know if he could trust love a second time.

"You're early."

The shocked voice caused him to look up from the label he was currently peeling off his beer bottle. He stood—or stumbled, truthfully—out of his chair to stand as Lilly tilted her head, glasses slipping down her nose only to be pushed back up again by a single finger.

"Um, yeah. I wanted to make sure I got here early. I've noticed parking in Denver can be a bit..."

"Tricky?" she offered helpfully.

"I was going to say a pain in the ass, but, yeah. Tricky works, too."

She laughed softly, the sound filling his chest, warming the coldness that had taken up residence the past few days. He missed that sound, and it was his own damn fault.

"Sit." He indicated the chair across from his. "Can I get you a drink?"

"Vodka cranberry, please."

As she took her seat, Lincoln hurried to the bar to place her order. The bleeps and bells of various arcade games filled his ears, muffled voices carrying bits and pieces of conversation as he waited with as much patience as he could muster. Once the bartender finished his order, he handed over some cash, enough to cover the drink and a hefty tip. Grabbing the pale red drink, he made his way back to the table, but Lilly wasn't there. Panic clutched his chest for a moment as he thought she'd changed her mind and taken off, but then his eyes scanned the barcade and he saw her, standing in front of one of the pinball games, hands on the flapper buttons, concentration fully on the game.

"Got your drink," he said as he approached her.

"Thank you," she acknowledged without looking up. She tilted her head to the side. "I brought your beer."

He looked at the small side table to see his beer bottle sitting there, slightly shredded label looking very telling of his current mood.

"Oh damn!" She slapped the game as her last ball slid down the side behind the bumpers.

The scoreboard displayed an impressive number, but he knew Lilly could do better. Seemed both of them were feeling off tonight.

She turned from the machine, bright green eyes staring him directly in the face. Challenging him. "Your game."

All right. He'd play.

He handed over her drink, taking up a position in front of the machine and feeding it a quarter. He focused on the game, watching the shiny silver ball whiz and fling up and down the ramps, banging against the flappers as he pressed the buttons, hitting sensor after sensor to tick his score higher and higher.

"So," Lilly said in his ear from her position behind his shoulder. "About what happened?"

His concentration broke, mind flying back to *that* morning, the warm bed, the sweet, comforting smell of her in his arms, the absolute disaster that followed. The ball sped down a ramp, sliding past the flappers into the depths of the machine.

She snorted as he cued up his next ball, pulling down the spring-loaded pin to give it a solid starting smack.

"You did that on purpose," he grumbled.

"Of course I did," she replied. "All's fair in love and pinball."

He swallowed at the word "love" but kept his focus on the game.

"Now, about your man-child freak out after I explained to you about what happened between the jerk and me?"

He gave her a quick glance over his shoulder. Quick,

because he knew she was trying to distract him from the game, and dammit, it was working.

"I did not have a man-child freak out. What the hell even is that?"

"It's when a grown-ass man hears something he doesn't like and decides to be all pouty and sulky about it. Like a child."

"I wasn't pouty."

"But you don't deny the sulky part?"

He let out a frustrated breath. "What do you want to know, Lilly?"

She was quiet for a moment. He heard the sucking sound of her straw before she answered him.

"I want to know why you acted the way you did. Why you acted like it was my—"

Her words cut off with a hitch. He abandoned his game to focus on the conversation, looking up to see her visibly blink back tears. Shit. He was the world's biggest asshole. He knew what she thought. That he blamed her. And yeah, maybe for a split second he had, but it was only a knee-jerk reaction. He'd had some time to think about things, and he knew his freezing her out at the wedding venue had been a dick move. Especially after all she shared with him.

Straightening his shoulders, he mentally prepared himself for the explanation he knew he had to give her.

"I was married." He paused, letting her take in that information. By the raising of her dark eyebrows, he'd surprised her. "Jessa, my ex-wife, worked at the local diner in the town where I used to live. After a few months of friendly flirting, I asked her out. She said yes, and we dated for about a year before I proposed. We got married eight months later."

Lilly nodded as if the timeline matched. He'd figured a year was long enough to get to know the person you wanted to spend the rest of your life with. He'd been wrong.

"We were married for two years before I found out she'd been cheating on me."

"Oh, Lincoln." Lilly's hand squeezed his arm, expression filling with pain. "That's awful."

He shrugged as if it hadn't ripped his fucking heart out at the time. "Yeah. I thought everything was going great. We'd even been talking about starting a family."

Thank God they hadn't.

"Then I accidentally grabbed her phone instead of mine one day and got a text from one of her fuck buddies."

"One?" Lilly asked, horror filling her face.

He scoffed. "Yeah. Evidently while she liked having a geeky computer husband to pay off the charges on her credit card, she preferred more...manly men to satisfy her sexual needs."

"What the hell does that mean?"

Lilly looked offended—for him. The sight calmed the ragged beast that always rose up when he talked about how his ex had duped him.

"It means she liked tough guys, bikers and jocks, but she also liked that I brought in enough money that she didn't have to work."

"That's awful."

He shrugged. "It was what it was. But it's over now."

Lilly stared at him, contemplating. "Is it?"

Grabbing his beer from the side table, he took a swig before answering. "Yes."

"Hmm." She nodded her head up and down, eyes narrowed, glasses slipping down her nose. She pushed them up again. "I don't think you've completely moved past it, Lincoln."

"I'm not still in love with my ex."

Her brows rose. "I never said you were. But I think you still hold on to the pain and betrayal, and it colors all your relationships now."

Did not.

"Answer me this," she continued at his silence. "When I first told you my story, how I found out I was the other woman. Did you, any small part of you, think of me as an adulterer?"

"No." The word rushed out of his mouth immediately, but the inflection must have been off, because Lilly tilted her head, studying him carefully.

"I might not have known I was sleeping with a married man at the time, but I was. His lies didn't change that fact, and for that I will always feel awful. Mostly for his poor wife, who was the most hurt in the situation."

He swallowed hard at her understanding.

"But I don't blame myself for what happened. Not anymore. And neither should you."

"I don't blame you, Lilly," he rushed to say. "I know you'd never do anything like that on purpose."

"Do you?" She shook her head. "I think you're still stuck in the past. Your ex did a number on you, and I can be sympathetic to that, but I'm not her. Not everyone is a liar. Not everyone leads strictly with their emotions, forgetting to let their brain into the mix."

She sighed, a sad smile taking over her soft features. "It took me a long time to figure that out. That the heart and the brain can work together. That you can have passion, love, and compatibility in a relationship. You just have to trust each other, be honest, and work out your problems before they become so big they crush you."

"But how—" He stopped as the words stuck in his throat, clearing it and trying again. "How do you know who to trust with…your heart?"

She stepped closer, grabbing his beer and setting their drinks down on the side table. Her hands slid up around his neck, delicate fingers playing with the long growth at the base. He needed to find a barber in Denver. An odd thought to pop in his mind at the current moment. But it vanished in an instant the moment she tilted her head up and placed a soft kiss to his lips.

"I think that's why it's called a leap of faith." She smiled. "Sometimes you just have to go for what feels right and hope you don't get hurt in the end, but even if you do, maybe you've learned something you never knew before."

He wanted to grab her, press her firmly against his body, and devour her lips, taste the sweetness of her mouth, swear he wasn't afraid and wanted to take the risk on her, on them. But he didn't. He was human enough to admit he was still scared shitless by the feelings she raised in him. Feelings he thought died after his divorce. No. Feelings much stronger than he'd ever felt for his ex. That's why they scared him so damn much.

What if he let himself fall for Lilly? Really fall. And the same thing happened? Maybe not the whole cheating thing, but what if they didn't work out? What if he gave his heart away a second time and it got trampled yet again? He didn't think he could stand that kind of heartache twice in a lifetime. His parents had decades of loving marriage, and he'd always thought that's what he would have, too, but he had failed. What made Lilly think he was worthy of her?

"Lincoln?"

Her soft voice made him realize he'd been staring into space for a solid minute, eyes focusing on the nothingness of the floor beneath them. A warm hand came up to cup his jaw, her fingers rubbing against the scruff of his beard. The softness of her skin should have contrasted with the hard prickliness of his own, but it didn't. Instead, he only felt comfort, caring, love. But his throat was closed off. No words could get past the fear clogging it.

"Okay." She kissed his cheek, stepping back, hand

dropping from his face.

He felt the removal of her body from his like a physical blow. The loss of her warmth left him chilled and anxious.

"I hope you find some happiness, Lincoln."

With a sad smile and a slight nod, she turned and headed out of the barcade. He stood there for a full five minutes, staring at the empty air she once occupied. It wasn't until someone nudged him, asking if the game was free, that he finally shook himself out of his stupor and moved aside.

He'd told her the truth, and it hadn't killed him. Even better, she'd understood—sympathized, even. She hadn't pitied him or blamed him for his reaction to her past. Lilly, like in all problems she faced, had simply worked for a solution and presented it to him.

A leap of faith.

Could he really do that? Open his heart while knowing it stood the risk of being destroyed once again? Letting go of the past was hard, and he thought he'd succeeded in doing just that, but maybe he hadn't. Perhaps he still carried around some anger and resentment about the whole situation. And who could blame him if he did? His wife, the person who vowed to honor, love, and remain faithful in sickness and in health, had lied. Done the opposite of everything she'd promised. Didn't he deserve to be a little wary when it came to matters of the heart?

Not that Lilly was in his heart...

He needed another drink. Good thing he was in a bar. He'd parked his car in an overnight lot, and he had a rideshare app on his phone. Before he had planned to down a few more beers, play some pinball, and clear his mind of all manner of love and feelings. Except playing pinball only made him think of Lilly, and he couldn't really appreciate the taste of beer in his current mood. What was the point?

The crowded bar scene was starting to suffocate him, so

Lincoln headed out into the cold night air, walking the three blocks to where his car was parked. Once he arrived at his apartment, he flipped on the TV. But the latest superhero show playing on the small screen did nothing to distract his whirling mind from the problem at hand.

He had promised himself he wouldn't fall in love again. The risk of heartbreak was just too much. His judgment had been wrong once before, his trust shattered. So why did he find himself believing Lilly, trusting her? He thought about what he knew of her, what he *really* knew. Sure, they hadn't known each other for very long, but he knew she was loyal to her friends, took pride in her job, would do anything to make her clients happy—even deny herself the thing she craved most because it went against her own moral code.

Hadn't she refused to hop back into bed with him once she discovered he was a part of the wedding party? As much as he knew she wanted to, Lilly hadn't budged until the wedding had been over. Until their time together would be clear on her conscience.

She made him smile and laugh and want…so much more than he ever thought he would. This shaky burn deep in his chest was something he'd felt once before but never thought he would feel ever again. And certainly never to this magnitude. It could only mean one thing.

He was in love. And scared shitless.

Chapter Twenty

"Okay, Mopey Melvin." Marie slid a cappuccino in front of Lincoln. "Time to fess up."

He glanced up from his computer, where he'd been working on finding a bug in the code he'd been assigned.

"Mopey Melvin?" He raised a brow. "Is that even a saying?"

The small woman shrugged. Pulling out the chair across from him, she sat. It was just after three in the afternoon on a Wednesday, and he was the only person in the shop except for the owners. A week and five days since the wedding, a week and four days since the amazing snowed-in day he shared with Lilly, and a week exactly since she accused him of living in the past and told him to figure his shit out. Not in those exact words, but the sentiment had been implied.

And here he was. A week later. With not a damn thing figured out.

"Why aren't you at work?" Marie asked.

He pointed to the computer in front of him. "I am. I'm working remotely this week. They're painting the fourth floor. All the devs are working from home."

Or a coffee shop, in his case. He hated to admit it, but his basement apartment had felt cold and lonely the past few days. Ridiculous, because there'd only ever been him living there. How could he miss a woman he'd never even had a relationship with? She'd never stepped foot inside his place. He shouldn't miss her while sitting on the barstools in his tiny kitchen. He shouldn't lament not hearing her laughter as he sat alone on his leather couch, watching some stupid TV show. He shouldn't ache to hold her in the darkness of night as he tossed and turned on his large queen-size bed, wishing she was there with him so he could kiss every inch of—

Okay, maybe the bed part made sense, but the rest didn't.

Why was Lilly in his mind twenty-four seven when they'd never even gone on a proper date?

Because I'm in love with her.

Damn! He'd promised himself he wouldn't go down that road again. Dating? Cool. Fun relationship? No problem. But serious love-type emotions? He wasn't doing that again.

"Okay." Marie tilted her head, silky, short black hair sliding over her cheek.

She pushed it back behind her ear with a single finger, the move reminding him of how Lilly always used a single finger to push her glasses up her nose. Dammit. Why did everything remind him of that woman? Even his best friend, whom he'd known a hell of a lot longer than Lilly.

"That answers question number two, but what about question number one? What's with the 'tude?"

"I don't have a 'tude."

"Kenneth!" Marie called over her shoulder.

From behind the counter, where he stood cleaning some weird piece of coffee equipment, Kenneth shrugged. "You got a 'tude, dude. Noticed it the second we got home from the honeymoon."

"What happened with her?"

He stared at Marie, conjuring up his best confused expression as he asked, "What happened with whom?"

His friend, wise to his bullshit, rolled her dark eyes. "Lilly."

Dammit.

"Why would you think anything happened with Lilly?"

"Oh please." Marie laughed. "You always smiled, big and bright, whenever you were around her. A real smile, not that fake toothy monstrosity you've been putting on for the past year. The sprinklers almost erupted due to the fireworks you two had during the dance class. Any time the woman's name is even mentioned, you get all puppy dog eyes."

He scowled. "I do not get puppy dog eyes. I don't even know what that means."

"It means you like her, dumbass. Maybe even *more than* like her."

"Hey!" He leaned to the side to call out to Kenneth. "Your wife just called me a dumbass."

"You are a dumbass," his buddy replied.

Marie nodded. "Especially if you let a great woman like Lilly slip away from you."

She wasn't slipping away. He'd pushed her away. And didn't that just make the entire situation even worse? Here he was, a divorcé who didn't believe in love, but did believe in commitment, but didn't want to commit his heart to anyone again. His logic was so screwed up he could barely follow it.

"Come on, Kenneth," he pleaded with his friend. "I thought you were against the whole Lilly-and-me thing?"

Kenneth rubbed the back of his neck, a slight grimace on his face. "Yeah, I'll admit I might have been thinking a little selfishly at the time. Ya know, didn't want you and our wedding planner messing around to screw up our day, but Lilly is great, man. Like, really great. I still can't believe the miracle she pulled off at the wedding. I thought the snow was going to ruin everything for sure. But she found a way to save everything. A woman who cares that much about other people's happiness is a keeper."

"You know what?" He closed his laptop. "I don't think I want to have this conversation right now."

He started to rise from his chair, but a hard glance and a finger point from Marie caused him to retake his seat.

"Too damn bad, Reid, because we're having it."

He placed his laptop in his bag, reaching for his coffee as he focused on his friend. "Okay. Say your piece, Marie."

"Thank you. I will." She cleared her throat, placing her hands on the table, one folded on top of the other. "Lincoln, you know how much Kenneth and I love you."

He did. They were the three amigos. Best friends through thick and thin.

"So," she continued, "it not only hurt you when Jessa cheated. It hurt us, too."

His jaw clenched at the mention of his ex and her infidelity, but he let his friend go on.

"Watching the pain and doubt you went through killed us. I wanted to find that bitch and rip her hair out strand by strand for what she did, but Kenneth wouldn't let me."

"You would have gone to jail, honey," Kenneth called from the counter. "Lincoln wouldn't have let you risk yourself like that, either."

Damn right he wouldn't. He loved his friends' loyalty, but he didn't need them to fight his battles. His lawyer had taken care of that when she made sure Lincoln didn't pay any alimony to his unfaithful ex.

"The point is, we hurt for you. And we were angry at Jessa for what she did. But when she left your life, she left ours, and eventually the anger faded. I know it's harder for you because you were the one who was in the actual marriage."

"I'm trying to get over it." He shrugged.

"Are you?" Her brow furrowed. "You haven't really

dated anyone since Jessa. You haven't even been interested in another person. Not until Lilly."

Shit. That was true. He hadn't wanted anyone after his divorce. Not until he'd caught the eyes of a beautiful brown-haired goddess at the hotel bar. Talked with her, laughed with her, made exciting, passionate love with her. To tell the truth, he'd been hooked on Lilly since night one. The morning he woke up to find her gone—no note, no last name, no number, no way of contacting her—he'd had a small ache in his chest. A whisper of lost opportunity, missed fate.

Then, when he saw her again in the meeting for Marie and Kenneth's wedding and he realized he would get to spend more time with her, the ache disappeared, only to be replaced with desire, longing, a single-minded determination to not waste the second chance fate had given him.

But then he'd gone and screwed it all up. And he wasn't sure how to fix it.

"I—" He cleared his throat when his voice cracked, emotions rising to the surface. "I don't know if I can do this again."

Marie tilted her head in confusion. "Do what?"

He remained silent for a moment, weighing the outcome of making his confession out loud. If he kept it in, he could go on ignoring it. Pretend it didn't exist and go back to his status quo. His life was perfectly satisfactory before Lilly came into it. He was certain he could live a long and relatively happy life going back to the way things were.

But he couldn't. Not really. And he knew it. You didn't go back into a dark cave once you saw the brilliance of the warm, bright sunshine. You didn't go back to butter on toast once you had the rich, velvety taste of cream cheese on a soft bagel. And he couldn't go back to his pleasant, easy life now that he knew the opulent vibrancy Lilly brought to his humble existence.

Blowing out a weary sigh, he looked his friend in the eyes and admitted the truth. "I don't know if I can take a risk on love again."

"Oh, sweetie. We all take a risk on love. All the time." Marie placed a hand on his. She glanced over her shoulder. "Kenneth and I know that every day we get is a gift. My cancer could come back at any moment and rip us away from each other."

"No." He shook his head. "You're fine. You've been in remission for over a year. It's gone now."

She smiled. A soft, sad tilt of her lips. "You're very sweet, but we both know that's not how it works."

"Life's a bitch, man."

He glanced up at Kenneth's words. The other man had come out from behind the counter at some point in the conversation Lincoln was having with his wife and made his way over to the table. Now he stood behind Marie, a supportive hand on her shoulder, but his attention was focused on Lincoln, expression serious.

"Don't think Marie and I haven't talked about what we would do if her cancer came back. We have. It's a possibility, but it's not a reality—at least not right now. And you have to live in the now. If you live in the land of possibility, always worrying about what might happen, who could get hurt, then you aren't really living at all."

"Thanks, Dr. Phil."

"Hey." Kenneth held his hands up. "I admitted I was wary of you and Lilly hooking up at first. And it wasn't just the wedding stuff. You two really don't seem to have a lot in common, and I didn't want you to get hurt again, but then I saw the way you look at her. The way she looks at you. I know what that look means, Lincoln. I'm living it."

He leaned down to kiss his wife on the forehead. "Also, my very intelligent wife explained to me that it's your life and if you don't start facing your fears and living it, you're going to regret what you could have had."

Marie reached up to squeeze her husband's hand. "Believe me, I know. I almost made the same mistake."

He wanted to be flippant. Ignore the harsh truths his best friends were dishing out and push everything way down deep like he'd been doing for the past two years. But they had a point. Ever since he and Jessa split up, he hadn't been living in the now. Sure, he'd moved on, moved out of their house into an apartment, eventually moved states and jobs, even convinced himself he could start dating again. But all of it had been surface-level stuff. All things to show he'd moved on when he really hadn't.

He didn't love his ex anymore. She'd destroyed their love with her betrayal. Maybe he had been too boring or whatever, but she could have come to him. Told him what she was feeling—hell, even asked for a divorce before stepping out on him. But she hadn't. She hadn't shared any of what she'd been feeling.

Lilly shared. She was the most honest person he'd ever met. The woman was fascinating, a dichotomy of buttoned-up civility and uninhibited passion. She commanded a room with a single look but held a world of compassion with nothing but a touch. She didn't take any shit, but she cared, deeply, for those around her. Honestly, she intimidated him a little. And he loved it. He loved her.

"Say that again?" Ken asked, letting Lincoln know he'd spoken his last thought out loud.

"I love her. Lilly." He shook his head. Finally saying it out loud astounded him even as it warmed the dark part of his heart he thought long dead. "I love Lilly."

"Hell, man. We know that. Anyone within five feet of you two knows that."

Marie laughed softly. "Yup. Even her friends want you two back together."

His eyes widened with shock, a small smile ticking up the corner of his mouth. "They do?"

"Yeah." Marie smiled. "Mo called me yesterday asking if she could bring some brownies over to the shop for you sometime this week."

His smile dropped, remembering Mo's earlier threat. "Do not eat those brownies!"

Marie reeled back at his fervent demand. "She hasn't brought them by yet. Why? Is she a bad cook?"

He had no idea, but knowing how close Lilly was to her friends—something they had in common—he was sure she'd told them all about his jackassery over the wedding weekend. He'd bet all the terabytes in the world Mo was making him the kind of brownies that would have him staking out in his bathroom for an entire week.

Oh boy, he had some serious groveling to do.

A thought occurred to him, and a smile curved his lips. "Hey, can you two help me with something?"

Marie crossed her arms. "Depends on what it is."

"Is it a plan to win back Lilly for whatever asinine thing you did to piss her off?" Kenneth asked, absently massaging his wife's shoulders.

He stared at his friends, at the love they shared. They'd faced one of the absolute worst things life could throw at a relationship. Marie stared death in the face and told it to fuck off. Okay, she didn't, because his sweet friend would never use that kind of language, but she did kick cancer's ass. She also opened her heart to Kenneth, allowed him to take some of her load. Trusted him to be by her side no matter what the future brought. She placed her faith in the person she loved, and Lincoln wanted to do the same with Lilly.

If she'd still have him.

Good thing he had a kick-ass plan to help with that.

"Yes," he answered. "I have a plan."

"It better involve a lot of groveling," Kenneth leaned over to not-so-silently whisper. "Women like it when you grovel."

Marie elbowed her husband in the stomach. "We like it when you boneheads admit you're wrong. The groveling is simply a perk."

Kenneth leaned down to kiss his wife's cheek.

"There will be groveling," he assured them. "And a present."

"Everybody likes presents," Marie pointed out while Kenneth nodded. "How can we help?"

He had the best friends in the whole wide world. They were there for him when he needed support or a swift kick in the ass. How the hell did he get so lucky?

Maybe life would smile a bit more on him and allow him to win back the heart of the woman he knew owned his.

"Okay, here's what I need."

Lincoln laid out his idea while his friends listened avidly, nodding here and there, assuring him they could help secure the item he needed. When a customer came in, Kenneth moved behind the counter to take their order while Marie headed to the back to catch up on some paperwork. Knowing he needed to finish up his workday, Lincoln pulled out his computer again, but while his fingers worked code, his mind whirled with all the possibilities before him.

Lilly could say no to anything further happening between them. She could think he wasn't worth the trouble or find his apology lacking. Or she could say yes, and they could start something amazing, which would either last a lifetime or burn out, leaving them both scarred. All the possibilities terrified him, but if he didn't at least try, then he'd just be stuck where he was. Going through life without really living, without passion, without aiming for true happiness.

He had to try. And if he failed…at least he wouldn't be left wondering.

Chapter Twenty-One

"Whose brilliant idea was it to walk to lunch?" Lilly complained as her sensible black leather pumps with two-inch heels slipped on yet another patch of icy sidewalk. "My toes are frozen. It can't be over twenty-eight out here."

"Hey." Mo shrugged, sliding an arm through hers to help keep Lilly steady on the slippery walkway. "You're the one who decided to wear heels today."

"It's a workday, Mo. I always wear heels."

"Ooooh, I miss heels," Pru lamented, taking Lilly's other arm. "I haven't worn heels since my fourth month of pregnancy. Even my wedding shoes were ballet flats. I swear I lost all ability to move in those things since the twins."

As her friends walked beside her in their sensible—but completely not work appropriate—snow boots, Lilly huddled deeper into her warm down coat, resisting the urge to hide her frozen nose in the thick scarf wound around her neck. If she did, the exhalation of her breath would only fog up her glasses and make the trek back to the office all the more difficult.

Why had she let Mo and Pru talk her into having lunch three blocks away at Cherry's Café? They should have just ordered something into the office. But her friends had been complaining lately that she'd been working too much. So what? Their busy season was coming up in a few months, and she wanted to be prepared.

Plus, she'd started to make arrangements for her mother and the latest fiancé to fly out to visit venues. She was actually looking forward to it. She knew she wouldn't really get the quality mother-daughter time she craved, but she'd learned something recently.

You couldn't change people. You could only change yourself.

Her mother was who she was, and Lilly could either accept and love her for it or carry on longing for a relationship that would never happen. Vanessa Walsh loved her daughter in her own way. It wasn't the way Lilly wanted, but you didn't get to control how people loved you or even if they did. You could only control your own emotions and actions. So Lilly was going to love her mother as always, help her with this wedding and most likely another one after, and focus on the relationships in her life that gave her as much love as she gave them.

Like her friends.

She'd thought, for a moment, that Lincoln might be included in that list, but sadly, a full week and a half after their talk at 1up, that didn't seem to be the case. As much as it hurt to know the man couldn't get over his past to be with her in the now, she had to thank him. Before Lincoln, she thought relationships were black and white. Passion or compatibility. One or the other. She assumed if you fell head over heels for someone, that fire would burn so bright it would eventually be snuffed out, leaving a trail of devastation in its path. She'd thought she needed to match up with a prospective partner on paper, check off boxes on a list.

Her time with Lincoln taught her you could have both, a wild driving need for each other and the calm comfort of just being together. As much as she wished they could continue exploring all that potential, she knew—just like with her mother—she couldn't push Lincoln to love her the way she wanted. The way she deserved. He either did or he didn't, and there was no use pining over him. All she could do was take what lessons from their time together she could and move on.

Any day now.

Someday soon.

Hopefully.

The wind picked up, blowing snow from a nearby parked car into her face. She sputtered, the cold flakes freezing her lips, the frozen bits of moisture hitting her glasses, starting to melt from the warmth radiating off her skin.

Fantastic! She was freezing her butt off, could barely walk on these icy death marches, and now she couldn't even see.

"Remind me why we went out to lunch again?" she grumbled, clutching her friends' arms, letting them navigate her toward their destination.

"Because you've been working nonstop for the past week and a half and you needed a midday mimosa to loosen you up."

"I'm fine, thank you very much. And there was hardly enough champagne in that orange juice to call it a mimosa," she replied to Mo. Or to her general direction. The snow had turned to slush, and now her glasses were making her vision all blurry. She lifted a shoulder, trying to clean a lens on the soft faux fur lining of her coat, but it just made everything worse. Now she was trying to see through blur and cheap imitation animal hairs.

"Let me help," Pru offered.

Her friend took her glasses, rendering Lilly almost blind.

Everything turned into one large, blurred, shapeless object with various colors. Thankfully, Mo still had a good hold on one of her arms. One friend led her down the sidewalk safely while the other cleaned her glasses before popping them back on her face. The world came into sharp focus once again, as did other things.

"Okay, you two are right. I have been a bit…focused lately."

"It's okay, sweetie." Pru slid an arm through Lilly's once again as they turned the corner, their building in sight. "We understand."

"I know you do."

Lilly stopped, forcing her friends to stop as well. She dropped their arms, clutching her hands in front of her as she prepared to do something that would make her extremely uncomfortable but that had to be done.

"Um, I know I'm not the best at expressing my emotions."

Mo snorted. Pru nudged her with an elbow, and the blond woman mimed zipping her lips.

"It's okay. I realize I don't always say or show how much I love you two, but I do. You've both been there for me countless times, giving me advice, a shoulder to cry on—"

"Threatening to send laxative brownies to guys who break your heart."

Her eyes widened as she stared at her roommate. "Mo, please tell me you didn't send Lincoln your special brownies?"

The woman spread out her hands innocently. "I said *threatening*, not delivering, and you didn't deny that he broke your heart, so I might have to—"

"No." She shook her head. "Please don't do that. Besides, he didn't break my heart. I've learned that no one can do anything to my heart but me. It's not broken, but it is a little sad. And it might stay that way for a while, but it will get better, because I have you two."

"Awww, look at you, Lil." Mo gave her a small shoulder nudge. "Getting all sappy and stuff."

"Canon in D" chimed in the air. Lilly searched through her coat pocket for her phone.

"It's me!" Mo exclaimed, holding up her cell phone.

Lilly glanced at Pru, who also had her phone in her hand, staring at the screen.

"Seriously?" She shook her head at her friends. "I thought we all agreed to change our text notification sound so we wouldn't be grabbing for our phones at the same time like a bunch of idiots."

"We did agree," Mo said as she read her message. "And then none of us changed our tone, assuming the other two would."

"I can't figure out how to change anything on this stupid phone," Lilly complained. "I can send texts and make calls, but otherwise I'm out. Technology hates me."

She turned to Pru, who raised her hands in the air.

"Don't look at me. I have two seven-month-olds at home. If it isn't related to food, poop, or playtime, it's not getting done."

When she glanced at Mo, the woman simply shrugged.

"What? I forgot. Anyway, we don't have time to argue about this right now. We have a very important delivery waiting for us at the office."

"We do?" She didn't remember anything scheduled to come in today. Had one of their brides ordered something to be delivered to the office?

"He's ready?" Pru grunted when Mo elbowed her. "I, uh, mean, it's ready?"

She glanced at her friends. They were acting very strangely. In fact, they'd been acting weird for the past few days, staring at her with odd smiles on their faces…even today's lunch seemed out of the ordinary. They almost always ordered in or one of them went to pick something up and bring it back to the office for lunch. They were up to something.

Guess the only way she was going to find out was to go back to the office and see what the mysterious package was.

They made their way down the sidewalk and into the building. At the first blast of the building's heat, Lilly sighed in relief. She wiggled her poor frozen toes, vowing to keep a pair of snow boots under her desk for any future lunches out.

"Here, let me take your coat."

Mo grabbed the shoulders of the garment. Lilly barely had time to unzip it before her roommate tugged it off her back.

"Um, thanks." And why couldn't that have waited until they got in their actual office?

"Did you want to fix your lipstick before we head inside?" Mo asked.

She glanced at her friend. What an odd question. "Why? Is it smeared from lunch?"

It shouldn't be. She spent a pretty penny on this supposed ever-wear lipstick that claimed twenty-four-hour coverage. It had never let her down before.

"No. It looks great. You always look great, Lil. But I have a mirror if you want to check—"

"Mo, can it. She's fine."

Pru gave Mo a knowing look with the shake of her head. Okay, now they were being super weird. What the hell was going on? And why was Moira insisting Lilly check her appearance? Yes, she prided herself on looking poised and polished for all their clients, but they didn't have any client meetings this afternoon. Otherwise she wouldn't have agreed to the ill-advised trip out to lunch.

"You're more than fine, Lilly." Mo smiled as they reached the office door. "You're perfect, and I don't think your heart is going to be sad for too much longer."

Tilting her head, she stared in confusion at her roommate. "Thank you?"

"Don't thank us." Mo pulled open the office door.

Lilly stepped inside, her jaw dropping wide as a majority of the open space in the room was now taken up by a very large zombie-themed pinball machine. It looked just like... But no, that was impossible. It couldn't be...

"What the...?" She moved around the machine, fingertips hovering over the clear glass covering the ramps, bumpers, and all the playable parts. She was almost afraid to touch it, like it might disappear if she did. "Why is there a pinball machine in our office?"

"Because your building's elevator is broken, and I can't lug that thing up the stairs to your apartment."

Her heart skipped a beat at the familiar voice. She turned to see Lincoln standing in the corner of the room. How had she missed him when she first came in? Could have something to do with the giant arcade game she was standing by.

"We'll just head upstairs to drop off these leftovers," Pru said, backing out the office door.

Mo scrunched up her nose, a confused expression on her face. "What leftovers?"

Pru sighed. "Come on, Mo. They need privacy."

"Aw, but I want to hear him grovel."

Lilly chuckled as Pru wrapped an arm around Mo's waist and the two left, but not before Mo gave her a wink and a thumbs-up. The second they were alone, she turned to Lincoln, who made his way over to her and now stood only inches away.

"Lincoln. This looks exactly like..."

He shrugged, a sheepish smile curling his lips. Lips she'd been desperately missing.

"I know. Kenneth and Marie said groveling goes better with a gift. So I asked Mo for your mother's number and—"

"You spoke to my mom? Why?"

He rubbed the back of his neck. "I, um, didn't know Curt's last name, and it's hard to do a search of someone without their last name."

He called her mother to get Curt's name. Why? She glanced back at the machine, the reason staring her in the face, taking up a significant portion of her office. Tears gathered in her eyes as she turned back to Lincoln to ask, "Then this really is his? The old pinball machine?"

He nodded. "You were right—the guy is really nice. When I told him about how much the machine meant to you, he was more than happy to send it your way. He lives in Wyoming now, so I had to rent a truck and drive up to get it." He reached into his pocket and pulled out a piece of paper. "And there's also this."

Lilly took the piece of paper, her fingers trembling as she glanced down at ten scrawled-out numbers.

"He said you can call him anytime if you want to catch up. Said leaving you was the only thing he regretted about the divorce." Lincoln grimaced. "He also said he had a large plot of land where no one would find a body if I ever hurt you."

Lilly laughed as she clutched the paper to her heart. If she ever considered anyone a father figure, it had been Curt. She couldn't believe Lincoln called her mother and her ex-stepfather just to find the most treasured thing of her childhood.

"You were right, Lilly."

He took a deep breath, staring at her hand on the glass, lifting his to trace along each of her fingers. One at a time. The touch of his hand, after so many days aching for it, made her body ignite and her heart clench.

"I was living in the past. I don't have feelings for my ex anymore, but I also never let go of what happened. I held on to the pain, the anger, like a shield. Used it to stop anyone else from getting too close. From being able to hurt me again. But then I met you."

"Lincoln—"

He lifted her hand, intertwining their fingers. The dark scruff of his beard looked longer. As if he hadn't trimmed it in a few days. His eyes stared into hers; she could see the distress in them, but she could also see something else. Something she didn't want to name for fear of being wrong but hoped she was right.

"Our past shapes us. It makes us who we are, but we get to choose how that happens. And I don't want my past to stop me from being with the woman I love."

A tear slid down her cheek. Her heart felt so full but wonderfully light in her chest, the heaviness of the past few weeks melting away with Lincoln's admission. A happy smile curled her lips as she choked back a relieved sob of joy.

"I love you. I have for a while now, but I was too afraid to admit it. Too scared to risk my heart again, and I'm sorry for the way I acted, for hurting you, for even the millisecond of doubt I let creep into my head because of what happened in the past. You're not my past, Lilly. You're my now and, I hope, my future. I love you."

More tears slipping from her eyes, she lifted a hand to wipe them away. "I love you, too."

"My groveling worked, then?"

She shook her head. "No. It was totally the pinball machine."

Lincoln laughed, placing a hand on her waist and tugging her into him so he could dip his head and claim her lips. Every inch of her body and soul cried out with joy at the feel of being in his arms again.

"Then I guess there's just one more question I have to ask you," Lincoln said when they finally came up for air.

"Oh really? And what's that?"

Still holding her hand, he went down on one knee. She sucked in a breath. Surely he couldn't be asking what she thought he was asking? They'd just admitted their feelings for each other, and while she could see a future with Lincoln, she didn't think now was the time to—

"Lilly Walsh, will you go on a date with me?"

She snorted, slapping her free hand over her mouth as the loud bark of relieved laughter left her. With all her primp and polish, all her rules and propriety, how funny that she fell for a man she hadn't even had a proper date with. Life really did go its own way. She was just happy she finally learned to go along with it.

"Yes, Lincoln Reid. I will go on a date with you."

He rose, taking her into his arms once more. "Now, what do you say we break in this machine? Winner chooses date night activities?"

She grinned. "You're on."

No matter who won the game, they'd both won each other, and really, that was all that mattered.

Epilogue

SIX MONTHS LATER

"I don't understand how one man can have so many computer parts." Lilly glanced at the fifth—no, sixth—box labeled *computer parts* Lincoln set down in their new living room. After six months of dating, Lincoln had surprised the heck out of her by asking her to move in with him. Since his tiny basement space wasn't ideal for two people, they'd gone on the apartment search and found a great place just a few blocks away from her old digs.

Who would have thought the man who months ago said he didn't do long-term would be the one to push for the next stage in their relationship? Lincoln had changed a lot in the past months, and so had she. They'd both had to learn how to compromise and try new things, but along with that came the joy of sharing what you loved with the person you loved. They didn't always agree—she still hated camping (peeing in the woods, no thank you), and no way in hell would he ever get her to drink a pumpkin spice latte, but she'd agreed to go

RVing as a compromise, and maybe he could convince her to try one pump of vanilla syrup in her coffee someday—but they'd both learned to open their eyes to new experiences. And open their hearts to each other.

"What is it with everyone commenting on how much computer stuff I have?" Lincoln grumbled as he came in behind her. "I'm a computer guy; of course I have a lot of spare parts. You should be grateful. If I recall, one of these boxes used to hold the extra RAM I installed in your new computer."

Pressing her lips to his cheek, Lilly smiled. "I am grateful and thank you, sweetie."

There was nothing better than having your very own company computer guy on call twenty-four seven.

"What's that?" She pointed to the box in his hands.

Lincoln grinned like a kid on Christmas. "My *D&D* books. Curt said he'd join our campaign."

A week after Lincoln gave her Curt's number, she'd called him up. It had been a bit scary reconnecting with a man she hadn't seen in years but still considered the closest thing she'd ever had to a father. Curt had been so happy to hear from her. They even scheduled a meetup when his family came to Denver for his youngest's debate tournament. It warmed her heart to know Curt had found love. His wife was a very sweet woman, and his two kids were a hilarious handful.

Lincoln had come for moral support, and when the two men discovered a love of RPGs, they had spent an hour geeking out. Now Curt was joining them via video chat for their monthly game. She knew Curt wasn't her real father, but in a small way, Lilly felt like she got her dad back again. All she had to do was suffer through pretending to be a half-elf bard on a quest for a magical flute.

She let out a small groan.

"You promised to try one campaign."

"And you promised to try one weekend skiing."

He shuddered. "If I break my leg, I expect full Florence Nightingale treatment."

Laughing, she took the box from his hands and placed it on the soft beige carpet of their new place. A new beginning with the man she loved. Wrapping her arms around his waist, she gazed up into his eyes, a wealth of love shining out from them. Love for her. Something that still amazed her every day she saw it.

"You won't break anything, but we can always play naughty nurse if you want."

Lincoln bent his head down, brushing his lips against hers as he whispered, "The only thing I want is you."

Her thoughts exactly. So many things had changed in the past year, and she knew there were more changes ahead. Marie had let it slip that Lincoln had been asking Kenneth for local jeweler recommendations. Lilly wasn't going to count her chickens before they hatched, but they had been talking a lot about the future and what they wanted. All she knew was as long as Lincoln was by her side, she was happy. He could propose today or ten years from now; it didn't matter.

As long as they were together. That's all she needed.

"The movers already put the pinball machine in the spare room." Lincoln bobbed his eyebrows. "Wanna play?"

She grinned. "Loser unpacks the kitchen."

"You're on."

And pinball. Lilly always needed pinball.

Acknowledgments

I'd like to thank Paul for letting me ask him a million questions about computer programming, any mistakes are mine alone.

A huge thanks to my agent Eva Scalzo and my editors Stacy Abrams and Judi Lauren for continuing on this Mile High Happiness journey and loving Lincoln and Lilly as much as I do. Also a big thank you to all the staff at Entangled Publishing for all their support and dedication on this book.

And to you, the reader. Thanks for letting my imaginary friends live in your hearts for a little while. I couldn't do this without you.

About the Author

Bestselling author Mariah Ankenman lives in the beautiful Rocky Mountains with her two rambunctious daughters and loving husband who provides ample inspiration for her heart-stopping heroes. Her books have been nominated for the prestigious RWA Golden Heart® and CRW Stiletto awards.

Whether she's writing hometown heroes or sexy supernaturals, Mariah loves to lose herself in a world of words. Her favorite thing about writing is when she can make someone's day a little brighter with one of her books.

Discover the **Mile High Happiness** *series...*

THE BEST FRIEND PROBLEM

Find love in unexpected places with these satisfying Lovestruck reads...

SEDUCED BY THE SOLDIER
a novel by Melia Alexander

Zandra York just got her big break photographing a project for an international travel magazine. But when her brother's overprotective best friend gets off the plane instead of her brother, she knows this won't end well. Special Forces instructor Blake Monroe would do anything for Jackson, but "babysit" Zandra when he's called away on a mission? C'mon. She's more trouble than he can handle—and far too tempting. But how can two people heading in opposite directions find love?

THREE DAY FIANCEE
an *Animal Attraction* novel by Marissa Clarke

Between helicopter pilot Taylor Blankenship's job, his dog, and his matchmaking grandmother, he has no time for anyone or anything—especially a woman. The job of New York City dog walker suits Caitlin Ramos perfectly while she preps for her CPA exam. Men suck. Especially her bossy, hot client with the Saint Bernard that thinks it's a lap dog. Offered a bargain she can't refuse, Caitlin finds herself playing the part of fiancée to Taylor. All she has to do is fake a relationship with Mr. Bossy Pants in front of his entire family and not lose her heart to a guy who turns out to be a lot more than she'd bargained for.

THE ATTRACTION EQUATION
a *Lover Undercover* novel by Kadie Scott

FBI agent Max Carter's life isn't conducive to relationships—not that it's stopping his matchmaking mama. To avoid yet another set-up, he announces he has a girlfriend. And now he's required to bring her to Christmas dinner. Good thing he caught his sexy neighbor down the hall sneaking a dog into their decidedly "no pets" building, because she's *exactly* the woman for the job…

ONE SEXY MISTAKE
a *Chase Brothers* novel by Sarah Ballance

Olivia Patton's all about her one-night stand with sexy hacker Grady Donovan—until an epic snowstorm shuts down the city and thwarts her morning-after escape. Now that they have to *talk*, all hell breaks loose. Grady and Olivia can't stand each other. If it wasn't his apartment, she'd shove him outside to freeze. But with all the blistering sexual tension flying around, a second night with the hacker might be exactly what she needs… if they don't kill each other first.

Made in the USA
Columbia, SC
20 August 2024